Shadows in the Fire

Jun 29. 11

EULENE WATKINS

Eulene Watkins

outskirtspress
DENVER, COLORADO

Outskirts Press, Inc.
http://www.outskirtspress.com

ISBN: 978-1-4787-2310-3

Outskirts Press and the "OP" logo are trademarks belonging to Outskirts Press, Inc.

PRINTED IN THE UNITED STATES OF AMERICA

I began writing when I was 13-years old. My dream was to write books, so I started many. This is my first finished work.

Special thanks to my daughter, Tami, who did the editing, losing out on many hours of a fun camp trip to complete it.

Thank you to my husband, Archie, a former cop, for his legal input. He listened patiently while I read half the story to him and had to wait three months for the finished product. Thank you for your encouragement and patience with me.

Last, I'd like to thank all my friends who have encouraged me over the years to 'just get it done.' Your encouragement finally paid off.

Shadows in the Fire credits and denials:

This is a work of fiction. Names, characters, and incidents are either a product of my imagination, or are used fictitiously and any resemblance to actual persons living or dead, business establishments or their locales is entirely coincidental.

However; I have used the historical Wallow Fire as a back drop for this book. In the summer of 2011, the Wallow Fire burned 532,086 acres of Arizona forests, making it the largest wildfire in Arizona history. I've tried to stick to the time line of evacuations and events during that time.

Apache County is one of two of the largest counties in Arizona; its sister, Navajo County being the other. The northern parts of both counties are Navajo Reservation.

If you look at a map of Arizona, you won't find Round Valley, but if you ask any resident of Springerville or Eagar, sister towns at this location, where they live, they will undoubtedly tell you Round Valley. I've taken some creative license and created Round Valley, Arizona for the sake of my story. It is both Springerville and Eagar, and a combination of every small town in the Southwest. The streets and landmarks are real as are several of the small towns within that area.

The county seat for Apache County is St. Johns, thirty miles north of Round Valley, as is the sheriff's office. There is a sub-station in Round Valley. However, for the sake of my story, the sheriff's office has been moved to Round Valley. Other than these few subtle changes, I have not messed with the geography of the area.

The view from Andee's front door is one I've gazed from countless times, in my mind. Her house location is a place where I have longed to build, just for the view.

Prologue

The tall, dark man kicked the tire on the rented Jeep Cherokee and cursed. There was nothing to do but change the tire himself. He looked down at his white shirt, black trousers and black shoes, now covered with dust.

Reaching into the back of the vehicle he pulled out the lug wrench and loosened the nuts on the spare tire carrier. When they were off, he gingerly pulled the tire off the bolts, careful not to soil his shirt or pants. He dropped the tire to the ground. Instead of a healthy bounce that usually resulted when one dropped a fully inflated tire onto a hard surface, he heard a dull, sickly thud. He cursed again and kicked at the flat spare.

He pulled a cellular phone from his pocket only to read "no service" across the LED window. "Stupid backwoods dump," he spat. What was he thinking, choosing this area instead of just driving out to the desert?

The wind kicked up dust devils on the road in front of him. It was too hot to sit in the jeep and too windy to stay outside. It was the week before Memorial Day Weekend. He stepped out onto the dusty dirt road again. Despite the slight snowfall from the week before, the dirt roads were dusty and dust devils kicked up across barren meadows. Upon entering the National Forest he'd seen several signs declaring fire danger 'Extreme." It was three miles to the nearest campground where he might get some help and at least another twenty back to town.

He looked disdainfully at the tire lying near the jeep. He returned to the rear of the jeep, released the latch and opened the back door. He loosened the nut that held the jack in place. Shoving it under the jeep he cursed again as he realized he could not place it under the housing to raise the jeep without putting his knees into the dirt and dust on the road.

Pulling a white handkerchief from his hip pocket he wiped his hands and frowned at the dirt that stained his hands and trousers. You'd think a rental place would check its vehicles and keep them in prime condition, including the tires! Another wave of anger washed over him.

The wheel of the jeep inched upward with each turn of the jack handle until it was almost clear. The man left it touching the ground and applied the lug wrench to each nut to loosen them. When they were all loose, he dropped the nuts onto the floor of the jeep and returned to the jack, working it until the tire cleared a couple of inches. He removed the tire and leaned it up against the side of the vehicle.

Should he start walking or wait for someone to come by? Neither option was attractive.

He'd about decided to hike toward the campground when he heard the low rumble of a vehicle some distance away. Sudden panic hit. Even after considering hitching a ride, if one should happen by, he felt the urge to run into forest of thick trees and hide until the vehicle passed. Common sense surfaced. Even three miles in the shoes he was wearing was asking for trouble. He'd take a chance. It was doubtful anyone would remember him. He had covered his little package with branches and pine needles. It would never be found. And if it was, animals would have destroyed any evidence he might have left behind, which he was very careful not to do. Besides it was at least two miles away as the crow flies, and on a different road all together.

He took a deep breath and leaned against the front fender of the jeep, watching the road from whence the vehicle approached. The sound of an engine chugging up the long grade just beyond his vision became clearer as he stood there.

Again, he fought the impulse to slip into the nearby trees and wait until they had passed, but the thoughts of walking helped him to stifle the urge. The fine green of a forest service fire engine became visible as it crested the rise.

The crew cab engine, with the numbers 62 lettered on the side, chugged to a stop beside him. Four passengers and the driver stared out at him. He mustered a weak smile and pushed away from the jeep.

"Boy am I glad to see you guys," he tried to sound happy. "I was beginning to think I was the only person on this road."

A young firefighter clambered out of the truck. He wore standard fire gear, minus the coat and helmet. "Looks like you got a flat," he said and grinned sheepishly as he realized how redundant his words sounded in view of the obvious.

The man appeared not to have noticed. "Actually, I have two flats," he said. "The spare is flat as well. Guess I should have checked them, but I figured a rental place would keep that stuff done."

"You'd think," the younger man replied, looking over the situation.

By this time the entire crew had exited the cab of the engine. There were five of them. The driver rounded the front of the cab, and spat brown spittle on the ground from a lip filled with snuff.

"If your spare is flat, I don't know what we can do to help you," the driver said.

The man thought quickly. "Well, I'm meeting some fishing buddies back at the campground, if you could give me a lift, I can get one of them to come back and we can take the wheels into town and get them fixed," the man said.

The driver shook his head. "No can do. We can't take passengers due to liabilities, and we don't have the room anyway, but I can call a service truck from town to bring you up a spare to get you back to town." The driver looked at his companions. They nodded agreement.

"I'd be obliged," the man said.

"I'm John Wilson," the younger man introduced himself and offered his hand to the man. "This is Steve Connors, Gwen Watson, Wendy Thompson, and Tom Sly."

The man cringed inwardly and forced a smile to his face. John Wilson reached inside the truck for his microphone to call dispatch.

"I didn't get your name," John Wilson said.

"Oh, ah, Roger," he said. "Ahm... Roger Smith."

"Nice to meet you, Roger Smith," Wilson grinned and related the information to the dispatcher.

The crew clambered back into their seats, and

buckled in. John spoke briefly to Roger Smith. "Someone will be along in about an hour. Have you got plenty of water?"

Roger looked sheepish. "Actually, I wasn't planning to be up here that long. I left without any."

John opened a cooler strapped to the back of the truck and extracted two bottles of water. He offered them to Smith. "These should last you 'til the service truck gets here. I'd stay in the jeep out of the wind as much as possible until they get here. The sun is mighty deceiving up here and it'll get to you faster than it will in the desert. Just open a window on the off side of the wind."

"Will do," Smith told him. "And thanks."

The engine rolled away with waves and wishes for good luck pouring out the windows from the five members of the engine crew.

He wanted to kick something again, but contained himself until they were out of sight. Uncapping one of the bottles of water, he turned it up and chugged it down. Then, with a curse, he turned and tossed the empty bottle as far as he could. As it left his hand he heard the voices of his wife, *"You know you shouldn't litter. It's not good for the environment."* He cursed again and kicked at a stone.

Chapter 1
Monday, May 30, 2011
A Wee Bit Of Mayberry

Deputy Bernadette Fite opened the door of her white Chevy Tahoe and stood momentarily beside it, while taking deep breaths and slowly exhaling. She listened to the irate male voice from within, sighed and turned quickly to open the back door of the caged area where the department hauled their prisoners. The man was a royal pain in the backside.

Good ole George just had to leave her with a loud-mouthed, belligerent, know-it-all while he finished his campground patrol. Memorial Day Weekend was the beginning of the summer festivities at the Gateway to the White Mountains of Arizona. July fourth had always been the big holiday for summer in the otherwise quiet little town. Up until last year, summer didn't really start until Independence Day.

However, this year some members of the Chamber of Commerce had traveled north to a small western town in Wyoming and brought back some different ideas about tourism. Night rodeos were scheduled every night during the week, and day rodeos on Saturday, which was a lot different than most years when rodeos usually took up two days in July and that was if it fell on a weekend.

Craft fairs were scheduled at least every other week throughout the summer, and at least two triathlons and a health fair to benefit the local hospital. Barbeques and street fairs filled the otherwise blank days on the calendar. The sleepy little town had come awake. Tourists had begun to filter in as far back as a week before.

Their efforts seemed to be paying off. Every motel, hotel, bed and breakfast and campground or trailer park in town was full and had been booked for the summer, as were the ones in neighboring towns. Horses, horse trailers, pickup trucks, red, white and blue flags, cowboys and cowgirls and a lot of *wannabe* cowboys, as well as tourists, crowded the streets of the little town.

Many of the visitors hadn't come to town for the rodeo hoorah. Many were camped at the various lakes that dotted the White Mountains to the south of town. The sheriff had put everyone on extra duty and campground patrol was considered a picnic compared to patrolling the town.

The only kink in the holiday seemed to be the incessant wind that hadn't let up since January, and indeed seemed to get worse as summer drew nearer. A light snow storm in the mountains the week before had kept the forest open for the Memorial weekend. The deputy wondered how the campers on the mountain were enjoying their windy stay. It certainly wasn't pleasant in town.

"Please step out, sir," she said to the man inside. "And watch your step." She stepped aside, away from the man as he emerged from the vehicle, with his hands cuffed behind him. He shrugged off her help. "This way sir," she directed politely, although her teeth were clinched and her expression grim.

"Be careful," she cautioned, as she grabbed his arm to guide him away from a large pile of soft, fresh horse manure lying on the pavement. The man jerked his arm away, growling at her to keep her hands off him. With his hands cuffed behind him, he lost his balance and teetered backwards. At a loss whether to try and save him from a nasty fall or risk another angry outburst, she watched helplessly as he lost his footing. He fell backwards on his rear end.

Bernie watched helplessly, and then covered her mouth to keep a giggle from erupting. She was glad she was standing behind him. He had landed in the freshly dumped pile of horse manure she had tried to steer him around. On the positive side, it had probably cushioned his fall and kept him from breaking his tailbone. *And could have been a messy wet cow pie,* she reasoned.

The man sputtered, looking around to see if anyone had witnessed his fall besides the deputy who was trying hard not to laugh.

"Well, don't just stand there, you stupid... stupid sheriff," he yelled. "Help me up," he demanded.

Well, at least he was taking George's orders seriously. He had called her some pretty ugly names out there on the road. George had warned him about his mouth and evidently he had taken the warning seriously.

Bernie grabbed his arm and hoisted him to his feet. He looked at her, somewhat startled at her strength. She guided him up the steps to the sheriff's office and hit the automatic door button. The heavy glass door swung open. Her prisoner preceded her into the cool interior of the sheriff's office.

"Oh, crap!" her prisoner exclaimed upon seeing the wooden barriers that separated the public from the rest of the office. At the end of the room, two jail cells were visible, complete with a single cot in each. "I've landed in Mayberry!" And indeed the room was somewhat reminiscent of the sheriff's office portrayed in the old television series Mayberry RFD. Except that there were no locks on the cell doors and each cell was a room in itself, complete with a solid door that could be closed for privacy. The bars on the outside simply added to the façade of jail cells. From the office the cells looked like jail cells, but upon closer inspection, one would find they were actually two finished rooms. Heavy black curtains draped the walls on the outside, with heavy bars over that. Even the doors that swung shut on the rooms were covered with a curtain and bars, but once the door was closed, the inside was a small bedroom of sorts. The deputies and sometimes out of town guests, used the rooms to catch up on some sleep when it wasn't prudent or timely advised to go home before going back on shift. The actual jail cells were in the back, along with booking and the restrooms. The sheriff and other personnel used the front cells and cots to rest whenever necessary.

The room had, at one time, been the offices for the local Forest Service and retained much of the old oak furnishings. An oak railing ran the full length of the room, providing a passageway to the public restrooms and separating the main room from two desks situated in the center of the room. A door opened at the far end of the room and the sheriff walked in.

"Everything okay, Bernie?"

"Sure," Bernie replied. "Mr. Mitchell, this is the sheriff." She paused for emphasis. "Sheriff Andee Taylor." She waited and watched, a half smile on her face, as the introduction sank in.

"You're shi…" he corrected himself, "You're kidding, right? Sheriff Andy Taylor and Deputy Barney Fife, isn't that the name that other guy called you."

The sheriff winked at her deputy. "Mr. Mitchell, was it? I'm the sheriff here, and my name is Andrea Taylor. People have always called me Andee. And it's Bernadette Fite, Bernie Fite not Barney Fife. But we kind of like the play on words." She wrinkled her nose. "Better check your shoes. It smells like you might have stepped in something out there on the street?"

Bernie checked a giggle, which resulted in a snort.

Mitchell threw her a look. *'That one was a killer,'* she thought.

"You think that's funny, don't you?" he growled. "Let's just get this over with so I can call my lawyer and get the h… get the …get out of here." *'George's warning was still in effect,'* she marveled.

"O.P. is in booking," Andee told her. "Sandra left for the afternoon."

Before Bernie could reply, Mitchell snorted. "This is too much. Sheriff Taylor, Deputy Fite and Opie! Good grief. You really don't expect anyone to take this hick town sheriff's office seriously?"

"Very seriously," Bernie cautioned him. She unlatched the swinging wooden barrier door and none too gently, steered her charge through it, motioning him ahead of her. She reached the end of the room, again touched an automatic door button and continued down the hall.

Sheriff Taylor watched them until the door closed and returned to her own office. She grinned wryly to herself. Maybe it was a little much, but Oliver Phillip Barry had been called O.P. all his life. His mother had refused to hang a junior on him or call him Little Oliver to distinguish him from his father Big Oliver. To most he was O.P., although some called him Ollie. Maybe she should call him Ollie. Except when the Mayberry façade was in place, she grinned.

And she really ought to hit the Board up about changing the interior of the office and update it with more security measures. They had shatter-proof glass on the door at the front of the building and automatic door openers, but once a person stepped inside, the quaintness of the office often brought remarks of Mayberry RFD. She chuckled. And now that she was Sheriff Andee Taylor, and the Good Lord had had the good humor to send her Deputy Bernie Fite, she really hated to spoil the picture. Besides she rather enjoyed the looks of astonishment every time someone saw her office and likened it to Mayberry. She

loved being able to tell them she was Sheriff Andee
Taylor with a deputy named Bernie Fite.

Not that Round Valley was anything like the
Mayberry portrayed in the television show. Quite the
contrary. It was a small modern town with a rural
attitude, on the east side of Arizona near the New
Mexico line. The nearest town to the north and
south was thirty miles and to the east and west was
fifty miles.

Andee had been the sheriff for just over a year.
She had campaigned hard to win the election from
the former sheriff, Hilton Parks, who had held the
office for over twenty years. She hated mudsling-
ing campaigns and vowed she would not stoop to
those tactics, even knowing that the whole county
would probably back her if she brought up some of
the former sheriff's public sins. But she didn't. She
ran a clean, positive campaign. She had commended
Sheriff Parks for cracking down on the drug traffick-
ing in the county and for busting several methamphetamine labs in his last year of service. She did not
mention the fact that until his son had been busted
for manufacturing and selling meth in the neighboring county; he had done very little in the way of drug
enforcement. Nor that the burglaries in some of the
outlying areas of the county had dropped to almost
nothing since his son had been imprisoned.

Not that the sheriff was responsible for his

grown son's actions. In court he had convinced a judge that he knew nothing of his son's activities, but there was still a question in most folks' minds about his innocence.

She had kept most of the deputies that worked for Hilton when she became sheriff. She thought that for the most part, they were all good officers. Two had quit outright the day she was sworn in, and she had let two others go, one with a recommendation, one without.

County regulations required she advertise for the positions. She had filled three of the empty spots when Bernadette Fite's application crossed her desk. Only two female officers had applied for the job. She had interviewed the first several days before and knew immediately the woman had lied on her application. A background check had verified most of what she suspected.

Bernie's resume' caught her attention immediately. She was a local girl. An expert in the martial arts, not that there was much call for that particular talent in this part of the world, but it showed a sense of discipline. She also was an expert marksman, scoring remarkably high with both rifle and handgun. Her academy marks were high and several of her instructors had written letters of recommendation.

She had enlisted in the Army National Guard at the age of twenty. Her enlistment was almost at an end when her unit was called up for a tour in Afghanistan. She reenlisted and did yet another tour, this time to Iraq before the aspects of war had put a damper on her wanderlust. When her tour ended, she had talked one of her brothers into recommending her for Law Enforcement Academy.

Her interview went well. Andee found herself warming to the slightly younger woman, and long after she had concluded the interview, the two talked far into the afternoon, finally ending up at the Sawmill Restaurant (a nostalgic place named for the Whiting sawmill that had operated at the south end of town for almost forty years) where they had supper together.

Bernie was a great disappointment to her mother, she told Andee. She was one of seven children, the only girl. Her mother had expected her to marry and give her lots of grandchildren. "When I joined the National Guard, she nearly went into hysterics," Bernie confided in her. "Then when we were called to Afghanistan and Iraq she really freaked out. When I got home from Iraq she had conned two of my brothers into inviting their single friends to our house for a backyard cookout. It was a nightmare," she said rolling her eyes upward and shrugging.

"So Mr. Right hasn't presented himself yet?" Andee asked.

"Uh uh," she said, almost choking on a French

fry. "I always said I wouldn't hook up with anyone I could outrun, outfight or outshoot. So far no one has come along who could best me." She shrugged. "Besides, one can always get married." She hesitated, "I'm an Old fashioned girl and once married," she shrugged, "a lifetime can stretch into forever if it's to the wrong man. I've seen it too many times. Broken marriages. Broken kids. Not for me. How about you?"

It was Andee's turn to contemplate an answer. "I don't know. I always thought I'd get married, just like my sister. But no one has ever come along that I could love and respect like my mom does my dad. Maybe I'm too picky, but my parents set some pretty high standards and not many men can hold a candle to that."

When they had parted company, Andee told Bernie, "As far as I'm concerned, you have the job. But the Board has to approve the hire. You'll be hearing from me one way or another."

She'd had to fight the Board, but in the end she had won. She suspected they had just wanted to throw some weight around to show the new sheriff they were in charge, but they couldn't pull anyone better qualified out of the stack of applications submitted and she needed someone yesterday.

A newspaper reporter covering the public board meeting picked up immediately on the Sheriff Andee Taylor and Deputy Bernie Fite and did a whole spread on the new sheriff and her new deputy, slanting the article in a way that questioned if a sheriff's office with this kind of tongue-in-cheek humor, could actually be taken seriously. Somehow the Associated Press picked up the story and it had gone national. The Chamber of Commerce had eaten it up, using the angle to boost tourism and advertise the present activities in town. There had been a steady stream of photograph and autograph seekers and both the sheriff and her deputy had obliged.

Andee stared out her window into the street as two young men and three young women dressed in jeans, boots and western hats passed by headed for the town's only mall. One of the young women pushed the man nearest her and he nearly toppled into the same pile of horse manure Mitchell had fallen into. She grinned and chewed her pen. She should get the scoop and go clean up the mess.

Bernie appeared at her door and tapped before stepping into the office. She grinned. "Guess I should go scoop some poop."

"I was just thinking that myself," Andee told her. "What's with the Mitchell character?"

"Drunk and disorderly. Ran off the road on the 260 near the Big Lake turn. I stopped to see if he needed assistance. He was pretty belligerent. I smelled alcohol on his breath and gave him a field sobriety, which he couldn't pass. I thought I'd have to put him down to get the handcuffs on him when I arrested him. Why do you think men, drunks in particular, think it makes them bigger and stronger if they yell and cuss and call a woman names?"

"Inferior complex, I guess. Pretty bad, huh?"

"Nothing I haven't heard before, but it still bugs me."

"I take it you didn't take him down?"

Bernie grinned and looked disappointed. "No. George came along on his way up for campground patrol. He must have made a believer out of the guy. He ranted and raved all the way to town, but didn't cuss at me even one time. He even corrected himself a couple of times."

"George has that affect on people now and then," Andee said. "Can't imagine why?" She grinned wryly.

George Townsend was well over 6 feet tall and weighed close to 280 pounds. A teammate had accidentally hit him in the face with a baseball bat during a high school game. The blow had flattened his nose and broken a cheek and jawbone. The bones had healed but not without leaving scars. His nose, flattened against his face had healed that way. He didn't work out in the gym. His strength came from hard work. He looked like a big burly gorilla and was intimidating to most people he met for the first time.

George's wife, Charlann, a petite woman from South Georgia, whom he had met while in the

Army, could not understand why anyone would think George was mean. To her he was, and had always been 'just George,' a hard-working, God-fearing man who was a good husband and father, a good provider, honest, and gentle.

"Did you have lunch?" Andee asked her deputy.

Bernie shook her head. "No, but I'm not hungry. I'll swing by the Mill later, or just do a Mickey Dee. I think I'll run out to the rodeo grounds and take a look around."

"Okay. I'm loaded with the paperwork Sandra left. I'm going to try to muddle through it. Then I'll take a drive around. Maybe I'll catch you at the Mill later."

"What's up with Sandra? Bernie asked. "It's not like her to leave the office early."

"Her mom took a turn for the worse. She drove over to Show Low to spend the afternoon with her. They think she might have had another stroke."

"I'm sorry to hear that. Let me know if you need anything. Or if Sandra needs anything." She turned to leave Andee's office. "I'll scoop the poop in front of the office. Next time it's O.P's turn." She flashed a big smile over her shoulder. Leaving the way she had come in, she picked up a huge snow shovel near the door and a five-gallon bucket.

Chapter 2
Not Your Regular P.I.

Andee balanced half a cup of coffee in one hand and a leather briefcase in the other as she closed and locked the door to her office. Taking the cup into the break room, she swallowed down the last dregs of coffee, washed her cup, and turned it upside down on the stainless drain rack at the edge of the sink.

O.P. had been in the break room again. The stainless steel sinks sparkled, as did their chrome faucets. The dishes had been put away in the tiny cupboard above the sink and the microwave smelled lemony. The floor had been freshly mopped and the wax glow he had applied the week before reflected the light from the overhead fixture. Not a crumb could be found on the table for four that adorned one corner of the room, even though just that morning they had all sat around the table drinking coffee and munching on breakfast burritos that Bernie's mom had made and sent them.

Andee smiled. She plopped her briefcase down on the table and picked up the cup she had just placed in the drainer. Taking a clean white towel from the rod above the sink, she dried the cup and placed it in the cupboard with the others. She smoothed the towel, folded it, and replaced it on the rod. That Ollie was going to make one heck of a husband when the time came.

She and others were surprised that the 35-year old deputy was still single. He'd been seeing Rachel Randolph, who worked at the Escudilla Real Estate Office, for a little over a year. There had been rumors of course, but he had remained noncommittal. Andee tried not to judge in these kinds of things, but she personally thought O.P. could do better. Not that Rachel wasn't nice. She was. Almost too nice, really. There was just something about that sugarcoated attitude that grated on her nerves. She shrugged. He was old enough to make up his own mind and make his own choices. Besides, the choices in Round Valley for a 35-year old man weren't all that great, nor, for that matter, for a woman.

On her way out of the office, she tapped on the glass-fronted door that housed the booking area. The deputy who had occupied her thoughts for the past few moments raised his head. When she waved her hand slightly and mouthed, "I'm leaving now," he grinned and gave her a thumbs-up and mouthed back, "Later."

The wind assaulted her as she moved away from the building. It always blew hard in the spring, but it seemed to be harder and to have lasted longer this year. Her Tahoe beeped as she unlocked it with her automatic opener. She wanted to leave it in the yard and take her own little Jeep Wrangler and drive up into the mountains and blow some cobwebs from her mind, dulled from hours of reports budgeting and balancing. She giggled, suddenly. *"Yes, Daddy,"* she said, as if he were sitting in the seat beside her. *"I know you said it wouldn't be easy. Well, I'm learning, aren't I? And I'm not complaining. Honest. I'm just tired and hungry, and I have at least five more hours before I can get some rest."*

In a sense, as sheriff, she had an eight-to-five job, unless something serious went down. Still, she had found it easier to stay out and available when the town was full. Otherwise she'd be called out anyway, so it was best not to settle in and have to wake herself up out of a stupor.

She backed out of the parking lot made a left on Mountain Avenue and turned right at the stop light on Main Street. She drove through town slowly.

At the 180 junction she turned right and picked up speed, driving south towards the rodeo grounds. She would check in with her deputies before going back to the Sawmill Restaurant for a bite to eat.

What a difference two years had made in her life. Two years ago, on the Fourth of July, she had spent the day at her parent's house for a backyard cookout. But two years ago, she wasn't sheriff, although she had been in the running. She had planned to spend the time up on the north end of the county campaigning, but her father had talked her into turning his own celebration into a campaign opportunity. As it turned out, attending the cookout had been a smart move, probably culminating a set of circumstances, which had won the election for her.

Her father, Ben Taylor, was a retired accountant and many of his accounts came from up north in Navajo Land. He'd spent many of his younger years building up the trust of the Native American population. He had become known throughout the county as a man of integrity. They knew him as a man who couldn't be swayed to bend the law, even if it cost him money. His clients learned early on not to cheat on their books or their taxes if Ben Taylor represented them.

A few well placed phone calls and some key people from Navajo Land had attended the cookout, met his daughter, listened to her platform, which sounded much like her father's own creed for life, discussed the relevant issues concerning their part of the county and left with bellies full, and their minds fixed on helping Ben Taylor's daughter become sheriff.

She had known going in that Sheriff Hilton Parks would not be an easy man to beat. He'd been sheriff of Apache County for twenty years and that alone gave him an edge. His son, Connie, had been convicted the year before elections for manufacturing and selling methamphetamine. Drug enforcement in Navajo County made the bust, finding and confiscating an operation with a street value of more than $2.3 million. Witnesses had implicated his father, the sheriff of Apache County, but nothing had actually been proven. Still, Andee felt that had helped her to win the election. Not that she had used it. But the suspicion was there and when the final count gave her seventy-five percent of the votes, she felt a certain sense of accomplishment and pride.

She turned the Tahoe into the entrance of the rodeo grounds. The gatekeepers saw the insignia on the side of her vehicle and waved her through. She parked next to two other department vehicles. Attaching the portable radio to the back of her belt and the microphone to the epaulet on her left shoulder, she slid out of the truck and gingerly picked her way through the horses, trailers, people and clumps of horse manure towards the grandstands.

Due to the winds, the rodeo turnout was not as good as they had hoped. Tried and true rodeo fans turned out, despite the wind, but those not accustomed to 50 mile per hour wind gusts tended to stay home and avoid the wind as much as possible. They could only hope that in true Round Valley fashion, the winds would die as the month of June progressed.

The announcer's voice boomed out over the speakers, "Ladies and gentlemen, cowgirls and cowboys keep your eye on chute four. Twenty-two year old champion bull rider, Stoney Whitehall will be riding Old Ruckus and in just a few minutes you'll see them bustin' out of that chute. You've all heard about Old Ruckus. He came into the rodeo circuit as a three year old bull and soon gained a reputation as a bull that couldn't be rode. Well, folks, Old Ruckus maintains that reputation. In the years he's been in the circuit, he's been rode once, and he…well, you all know the story of Randy Treselle and how he ended up being trampled by Old Ruckus. Randy's in the audience today. Good to see you Randy."

The audience turned towards the grandstands and applauded a young man in a wheel chair. He waved to everyone, and then the announcer drew their attention back to the bull riders.

"You ready, Stoney?" Evidently he received an affirmative response because he continued just as Andee reached the arena. "Ladies and gentlemen, Stoney Whitehall and Old Ruckus. Let 'er go boys."

The gate on chute four swung back and a big, brownish black, Brahma bull hit the arena head down, twisting, turning and kicking, tossing the rider on his back around like a floppy rag doll. Stoney Whitehall was everyone's favorite bull rider. A local boy who'd been lucky enough to make it to the big time and not be killed by one of the bulls he so loved to ride.

Andee felt her knuckles turn white as they gripped the fence. Bull riding was an event she both loved and hated. There was something about the stomach churning, edge of your seat, or corral fence, if you will, feeling that came over her that made her keep going back for more, while the other part of her wanted to close her eyes and shut out the possible and eventual consequences as bull became the conqueror and the rider hit the ground, dodging those sharp hooves and twisting turning head, sometimes mounted with long pointed horns that could toss a man ten feet into the air and spear his body through as he came down.

Stoney Whitehall lost his grip and his seat at 7.326 seconds. As Stoney hit the ground, the clowns moved in to distract the bull that was snorting and pawing the ground. Next to the bull riding, the clowns were her favorite part of a rodeo. She laughed with the crowd as Old Ruckus charged at a clown wearing blue and yellow striped balloon pants, and a bright orange shirt with exaggerated shoulder pads and waving a red flag. The timing was just right. The bull was within inches of the clown when he dove into a rubberized barrel. Old Ruckus butted it and tossed it in the air.

Andee relaxed and turned away from the gate, searching the edges of the arena for Bernie. She finally spotted her just to the left of the grandstand, near one of the concession booths. She was leaning on the fence and talking to a tall cowboy wearing a red shirt.

Andee began walking towards the concession stand, watching Bernie as she walked. Was Bernie talking business or was this something personal that shouldn't be interrupted? Andee smiled inwardly. *"Ever the romantic,"* she chided herself. She had just about decided to return to her fence rail when Bernie turned away from the cowboy. She waved slightly, shoved away from the fence, and with a few last words to the cowboy walked hurriedly towards Andee.

She wore a look that Andee had come to recognize as *'troublesome.'* When she was within hearing distance Andee called, "Hey Bernie!"

Bernie stopped short, glancing around to see who was calling her name before settling her gaze on Andee. She immediately flashed a smile and continued to walk.

"What's going on? You have one of those 'looks.'"

"I'm not sure." Bernie shrugged. "Maybe nothing. You want to get a hot dog or go over to the Mill where we can talk?"

Andee shuddered. "Ugh, no hotdogs for me. If everything is quiet here, let's just go over to the Mill. Is Brian still here? I saw his truck when I parked."

"Yeah, I think. He was talking to a couple of barrel racers earlier. Said he would be here till it was over."

They drove in their respective vehicles and parked at the Sawmill Restaurant. Andee called their location to dispatch. They walked in together and found a secluded table near the kitchen. It was a favorite table for most of the police officers in the area. They could talk over business without being overheard, and because it was so near the kitchen they received excellent service. Many times if the wait staff was busy with other customers, the cook or one of the other staff would bring them their meal piping hot from the kitchen.

Their waiter turned out to be Jason Stout, a fresh-faced fifteen-year old who looked nine and told most of his customers, especially little old ladies who thought he was *sooo* cute, that he was just eleven. He told them he was working to help his mom out because his drunken father had deserted them (his mom, himself and five sisters), two years previously. Which was totally false. Jason's father owned the hardware store, had never touched alcohol and Jason had one brother five years younger, who already was taller than him. The little bugger raked in twice the tips the other wait staff did. Andee admired his gumption, even if it was a bit dishonest. The little old ladies were charmed, and he socked his tips into a bank account to buy an airplane.

The locals all knew of his passion for airplanes. He was Round Valley's youngest airplane mechanic and as soon as he turned sixteen he would get his student pilot's certification. When he wasn't waiting tables or helping his dad at the store, he could be found at the airport, watching the planes take off and land or helping someone as they puttered around their own plane. He was on a first name basis with most of the pilots and all the mechanics and probably could take an engine apart and put it back together again with his eyes closed. Everyone teased him that if he could just find a cloud to park it on he could do it in the air.

"Hey, Jason, what's good tonight?" Bernie asked.

"Becky's running barbeque ribs tonight," Jason told them. "Best on the mountain, as you well know. Served up with buttered asparagus and fruit. Plus your own personal bib and lots of paper napkins," he grinned.

"Sounds good to me," Andee told him, handing him the menu. "And iced tea, then coffee after the meal."

Bernie nodded. "Make it two all the way."

"So what's up with the cowboy?" Andee asked her when Jason left the table.

"The cowboy?" Bernie started, "Oh, you mean Morgan Freeman? He's a friend of the family. He's working on an abduction case and thinks it might be connected to an identity theft ring down in Phoenix. Said he has reason to believe the thieves may be in these parts."

"He's a cop?"

"Used to be, down in Phoenix. He went through the academy, worked for the Phoenix Police Department, and the Maricopa Sheriff's Office, but after a couple of years on the street, he gave it up. Said he'd rather herd cows than get shot by some lunatic on the freeway. He does some private investigations stuff now."

"Okay," Andee grinned. "That tells me what he does, now who is he?"

"Just a friend of the family, really. He was in the Marines with Jake and then went to police academy with Jake and Sam." Jake and Sam were two of her six brothers. Three of them, Jake, Sam and Alan were cops, scattered across Arizona, working for different agencies. "He owns a small ranch over by Vernon."

She paused when Jason brought their tea with extra lemons in a bowl. She smiled at him. "Good boy." They always drank their iced tea with extra lemons. Jason was the only one who brought it to them without having to be asked.

Jason grinned. "Ladies, your dinner will be here shortly. Meanwhile, if you need anything… I'll check back in a little while."

"Thanks, Jason. We're fine for now," she told him. Jason flashed them a smile, and turned toward a couple two tables away.

"He said the case is turning out to be bigger than he had thought. He was wondering if we'd had any recent reports of stolen identity in the area. He wants to come by and talk to you after the town quiets down some.

"Seriously, though, Andee, he's a straight shooter. I have Jake's word. Next to me," she grinned impishly, "he said Morgan is the man to have in a foxhole. He can be trusted in a crunch. And you know Jake wouldn't give his approval if it weren't warranted.

"And I know how you feel about P.I.s since that sleazy Ratliff started poking around, but Morgan is nothing like that," she continued. "Give him a chance."

Andee shrugged. Bernie was right. She shouldn't judge all P.I.'s by Ramsey Ratliff. He was the definition of sleaze. He had poked around in her private affairs during her campaign for sheriff trying to find some dirt to use against her. She had always believed Hilton Parks had hired him. Nothing had come of it. She was glad she had resisted the normal drugs and alcohol temptations that hit teens and college students. In that aspect, her reputation was squeaky clean. *'Thank goodness they couldn't investigate her heart and thoughts. That may well have been another story,'* she often thought. She had never done drugs of any kind. She had attended church nearly every Sunday for most of her life. She'd never had an affair, or even the suggestion of a serious relationship.

"So what's up with this identity theft thing?" she asked.

"He didn't say much. A couple of people went missing down in the Phoenix area about a month back. Then just last week a credit card of one of the missing person's was used in the Show Low area.

Jason brought them a basket of homemade bread, another of Becky, the cook's, specialties, which they dove into immediately.

Andee broke a roll apart and spread it with butter. After taking a bite she rolled her eyes and gave Jason a big smile.

"This is to die for." He grinned at her, bowed extravagantly and left their table.

"Anyway, that's only half of it. Morgan said there had been several break-ins at some of the businesses, in the past six months. They were mortuaries mostly, in the Gilbert and Peoria area and the police think personal files and social security numbers were the targets. Then about a month ago, two secretaries for two different mortuaries disappeared."

"So the police are thinking an inside job maybe, or kidnapping?" Andee asked.

"That's just the thing," Bernie said. "One of the women was in her late forties. She'd worked for the company for fifteen years or more. The employer said she was honest and reliable. She was a new grandmother. He said she was beyond reproach.

"The other was seventeen. A senior in high school. She had worked at the same place every summer since she was a freshman.

"But get this, Andee, Morgan said there was an attempted abduction of an employee at another funeral home. The men wore masks and knocked her out, so she couldn't give a helpful description. That was just two days after the last two disappeared. And then another woman turned up missing shortly after that. He thinks the disappearances and the attempted abduction are related."

She looked up as Jason brought their ribs, complete with plastic bibs and a basket laden with red, white, and blue paper napkins.

"This looks delicious, Jason," she told him with a smile.

He grinned impishly. "It's as good as it looks. I took the liberty of sampling your plates before I served them. You know how that Becky is back there in the kitchen." He shook his head. "You just can't trust a skinny cook, you know."

They laughed at him as he had intended. He always joked that he sampled customer's plates to ensure their goodness or to keep from starving, because his "mean ole boss" (who happened to be his grandmother) wouldn't feed him.

He backed away from the table. "I will bring you ladies some more iced tea. Can I get you anything else?"

"Maybe some more bread," Bernie smiled at him. "And make sure it's fresh Jason," she said, playing along with his charade. "You probably should taste it. I don't know what's gotten into Becky. This last was a little stale."

"Of course, ma'am." He flashed another imp-ish grin.

When he had left their table, Andee picked up one of the beef ribs with both hands and bit into it. She rolled her eyes heavenward. "Becky out-did her-self today. Umm…mm this is good. My mom is go-ing to kill me. I was supposed to stop by for some supper at her house. I know I am going to pig out on this and I won't feel like eating more."

Bernie laughed. "Are you kidding? You can never be too full for your mom's cooking."

Andee scrunched her face. "I know. Maybe I'll just have dessert. I think she was making cherry cob-bler. The cherry trees are full of fruit this year. I think she's trying to get rid of last year's lot."

"Maybe I'll tag along with you," Bernie said. "I love your mom's pies. Maybe she'll feel sorry for me and send one home with me."

"Ah, so that's how it is. Bet you're right," Andee agreed. "Maybe if I whine when she gives you one, she'll give me one too."

They ate in silence for a few moments. Andee wiped her mouth with a napkin, and sipped her tea. "I dread the day when my metabolism slows down and I have to start watching what I eat."

Bernie nodded in agreement. They were both tall. Andee was five feet seven inches in her stocking feet. Bernie had a couple of inches on her, being just an inch short of six feet. Andee probably topped the scales at one hundred thirty pounds, making her mother fret often about how she needed some meat on her bones. Bernie, being the taller weighed one sixty five. She had large shoulders and powerful arms, but they were so well proportioned people were surprised at her strength. They both had long legs, which looked very good in their black uniform pants.

Andee's short, curly hair was an ash brown without the help of chemicals. She had a scattering of freckles across her nose, clear, blue eyes and long dark eye lashes, that required little, if any, make up. Her mouth was wide and turned up at the corners, which often gave the impression that she was secretly smiling about something and had gotten her into trouble on more than one occasion.

Bernie's Hispanic background, on her mother's side, contributed her thick dark hair, which she wore in a single braid down her back. She had her Mexican mother's clear dark skin but her Swiss father had contributed eyes that were neither brown nor green but a combination of both colors. Her face sported high, cheekbones and to her dismay, three dimples, two in her right cheek and one in the left.

When alone each received her share of admiring looks, but when they were together, more than one young man had tripped over his own feet while doing a double take at their individual and combined beauty.

"So this Freestone guy thinks the disappearances and the attempted abduction are related?"

"It's Freeman and yeah, he seems to think they might be tied in. He wants the sheriff's office in the loop, just in case. Besides, we have ways and means of running things down that a P.I. doesn't have."

"So he's being charitable so he can use our resources?"

"Andee," Bernie protested. "I told you, he's not like that at all."

"I know you said that. But I can't help being suspicious. I guess I just read too many books where the P.I.s are like Ramsey Ratliff."

"Well, reserve judgment until you meet him, okay?"

Andee nodded with her mouth full. When she had swallowed, she agreed. "That sounds fair. I'm looking forward to meeting your Morgan Freestone, P.I."

Bernie laughed, "It's Morgan Freeman, P.I."

"Beg pardon, Deputy Fite. Freeman P.I." She took another bite of rib and giggled.

Chapter 3
Thursday, June 2, 2011

It's Bigger Than
We Thought

Amy Holland paced the floor of the Big Lake fire lookout tower. This was her seventh year as a fire lookout for the United States Forest Service. She loved her job. The vistas from her tower gave her a start every time she looked out of the circular enclosure. But it was the rainy season she liked most of all. There is nothing quite like a mountain storm. Storms usually rolled in from the south with huge thunderheads building up on the horizon and then moving across the sky until everything took on a dark and eerie look. Then the lightning would streak across the sky, followed shortly by a crack of thunder, sometimes so close that the lightning hadn't cleared until the thunder vibrated her little tower room. Those also were the days when she couldn't leave to go home until the lightning had subsided, as the steps down to the ground were metal and she had no desire to be electrocuted. Monsoon was still a month away. If they were lucky, there wouldn't be any wildfires started in the next five weeks. Once the rains started, fire danger dropped significantly.

Today the wind was blowing and the tower swayed constantly. Her wind gauge measured 60 mph winds with gusts up to 95 mph at times. This was not her favorite weather.

The U.S. Forest Service had not closed the forest for Memorial Day Weekend, although fire danger measured extreme. There had been a small dusting of snow at the lower elevations earlier in the week, with slightly higher accumulations at the higher elevations. That was one of the contributing factors to no restrictions for this first weekend of summer.

Amy had already called in two smokes this weekend and a fire to the south had been named The Wallow Fire, as it had started in the Bear Wallow Wilderness area some time Sunday morning. They had hoped it would blow into the previous year's burn and burn itself out, but it had taken a different direction and was spreading fast.

Her radio crackled and she listened to the traffic between a lookout to the south of her tower and dispatch. She quickly picked up her binoculars and began to scour the southern horizon. The wind was pushing the fire fast. If it wasn't contained soon, it was going to be a really nasty one.

Amy had made her bed in her little loft. She would get up several times a night to check the fire blazing south of her tower. She normally didn't stay at the tower, but drove home to Round Valley every night and made the trek back up each morning. Tonight was different. Memorial Weekend was over. Most of the weekend campers had gone, but a few remained, scattered throughout the forest. She wanted to keep a watch on the Wallow blaze. Not that she could do anything about it, but knowing its position made her feel better. She made her way down the metal stairway and locked the gate at the bottom of the steps. She retraced her steps and dropped the trap door in the floor of the little enclosure, fastening the locks. She then moved a heavy work chest across the top for added security.

She wasn't afraid to stay by herself. She was alone most of the time, but there had been a few guests who had given her the willies, and given the time it would take for help to arrive should she need it, she decided not to take any chances.

Taking one last look around, she stood and watched the area south of her tower. Several ridges separated her from the fire, but the glow from its flames made it seem closer.

She picked up her microphone and signed off the air with her dispatcher, informing him of her intentions to stay at the tower for the night. She turned the knob on her gas lantern, leaving her little haven in total darkness. She left the radio turned on, but lowered the volume. It would be a long night, but even with that dreaded knowledge, a small flutter of excitement stirred in her stomach. Lying down on her cot, she closed her eyes and listened to the wind.

———⸺◉⸺———

Andee thanked her dispatcher and hung up the phone. Her deputies were already working in close conjunction with the fire authorities on the Wallow Fire. The fire was racing closer and closer to the village of Alpine, thirty miles south of Round Valley. Areas of the Blue River, south of Alpine and bordering the New Mexico line also had been alerted and evacuated.

She and Bernie had spent the early part of the evening making a presence at the three bars in town and at the rodeo grounds where a dance was going on. "Half the job of law enforcement is being visible," an instructor at the academy had told them. "The presence of a law officer is a bigger deterrent to crime than burglar alarms," he told the class.

As a result of that lesson, Andee insisted her deputies stayed out of the office except to write their reports and when investigations required phones. The rest of the time she wanted them cruising and taking calls. She didn't have enough deputies to have twenty-four hour coverage everywhere without overtime and the board frowned on that, but someone was on call at all times and she expected their *ready* response time to be less than ten minutes.

She smiled, remembering the surprise drills. She had worked it out with the dispatchers and then announced to all the deputies that drills would take place at intervals during the day and night in the next three months. In these drills the dispatch would draw a name from a hat and call that deputy and the sheriff. No one, not even the sheriff would know until they had both checked in 10-8 whether it was a true call or part of the drill.

The rule was that they both had to be dressed in full uniform and ready to take a call when they checked in. To date no one had beaten Andee's time, but Bernie and Edison Palmer had come close.

They still had drills on occasion, just to keep everyone, including the sheriff, on their toes. Tonight was not a good night for a drill she decided and picked up the phone to call dispatch. She then called Bernie's cell phone to give her an update and told her to pass the word along.

"Just what we need," she said to Bernie. "As if a town full of tourists, cowboys, and girls wanting to make time with cowboys isn't hot enough, we get a wildfire to boot. Remind me again how I love this job. And don't remind me that I actually worked my tail off to get it, either."

"Ah, you love it boss," Bernie told her. "Are you coming back out?"

"Of course, you don't think I'm going to let you have all the fun, do you?"

"Didn't think you would. I'll meet you at Circle K around midnight if we don't hook up before then."

Andee agreed and hung up the phone. She turned the lights off in her office and checked to make sure everything was okay in the jail area. Of the five cells in the jail area, two were occupied. The judge had released Mitchell and another man charged with DUI had taken his place. The other occupant was a man arrested in a domestic dispute. O.P. Barry had gone home and Clyde Walsh was on duty. He gave her a thumbs-up, indicating that all was well.

She checked in with the dispatcher and pulled out of the parking area.

An hour and a half later she pulled into the Circle K at the east end of town. Bernie pulled in a few seconds later followed by Edison Palmer.

"Hey, Ed," Andee greeted her deputy. "Anything other than the fire going on?"

The deputy grinned and shook her hand. "Not yet. I'm a little surprised. A lot of people in town, but the fire is the big news. I hear they are talking about evacuating Alpine tomorrow."

"That's the word I just got. You and Bernie are covering that, right? I think Nutrioso will be next."

Edison nodded.

He was in his early fifties. His thick, wavy, dark hair was tinged with gray around the temples and lightly silvered in the back. He was a stocky six feet tall with twinkling blue eyes. Andee had known him all her life. Rumor was that at one time he had been in love with her mother. He remained good friends with her parents, so if the rumor was true, Andee surmised there had been no hard feelings over her father winning favor.

Edison was just a few short years away from retirement. He had been widowed at the age of thirty-five with a teenage son. Rodney had been a disappointment to his father. Soon after his mother's death he ventured into the drug scene. As soon as he turned 18, he hitchhiked as far as Las Vegas, Nevada.

A short time later he married his young pregnant girlfriend. The baby was only three months old when she had died in a car-pedestrian accident, leaving the young man with a son whom he had no clue how to care for.

Edison had brought them both home, but Rodney soon became bored with small town life and returned to Vegas, leaving the baby with his father. That was seven years ago. Edison was devoted to his grandson Colin.

They helped themselves to coffee, paid for it, and moved to the back of the store to red plastic tables and chairs.

"How is the campground area looking on the mountain?" Andee asked Bernie. "Have they been evacuated?"

"For the most part, George has been running campground patrol. They'll hit the camps near Big Lake tomorrow. I think most of the campers cleared out after the holiday, but there are still a few camped up there. And of course, we have those who are determined to stay, no matter what. You know how people are. Check the site in the morning and someone has moved in before nightfall."

"Have they determined if the fire was human caused?" Bernie asked.

"Dispatch said possible lightning strike," Andee

replied. "I wasn't aware there had been any lightning storms, but the fire's origin is quite a ways to the south. It could be.

"There is a big mountain between it and both lookout towers in that area, so it wasn't sighted until it had grown pretty big. Since it started in the wilderness area, they couldn't do much about it at first. Besides ground couldn't get in there because of the terrain. They have a couple of hotshot crews on it as well as the planes.

"Copeland is on regular duty so once things die down here in *Mayberry*, you guys get some rest. Be prepared to get started first thing in the morning."

Edison laughed. "You been getting flack about the Mayberry thing again?"

Andee shrugged and Bernie choked on her coffee trying not to laugh. Together they related the story of Bernie's drunk and disorderly.

"If I know you," Edison looked pointedly at Bernie, "you probably pushed the guy down in that manure."

Bernie tried pouting but an impetuous dimple ruined the whole effect. "I truly wanted to, and believe me if I'd thought about it before it actually happened, I might have tripped him head first into it."

"For shame," Edison teased her. "And I've been telling everyone what a nice young woman you are."

"Really, Ed? You tell people I'm nice. You're sweet. Am I as nice as Miss Bethany?"

Edison grinned and lowered his head in embarrassment. Bethany was a waitress at the Sawmill Restaurant. He had been seeing her off and on for three years. She lived with her widowed mother who had quite a few health problems.

Edison recovered and socked her jaw in a playful manner.

"Apache-1, Dispatch," the dispatcher on the radio interrupted.

Andee keyed the mike on her epaulet. "This is Apache-1, go ahead dispatch."

"We have a report of a domestic disturbance at one of the camp trailers at the rodeo grounds. Section three, third trailer, second row."

"Ten-four," Andee replied and stood up, taking her coffee cup with her. "Guess we'd better roll." She dropped her cup in the trash as they called their goodbyes to the clerk and left the building.

Chapter 4

Thursday, June 2, 2011

Are We Lost?

"Wow that fire is a big one! And the smoke is getting thick up here, too," eleven-year old Jamie Porter called to his friend Steven Young. Jamie watched as his friend rubbed his eyes from the sting of the smoke.

"We'd better get moving. We'll be grounded for life it they tell us to move from camp and we're no-where around."

The two boys were about three miles from the overflow campground just off the FS68 Road that lay just south of Big Lake. They had ridden bicycles up the road from where they were camped, hidden them in the brush off the side of the road and hiked up an old logging road they had observed earlier. Jamie had talked his parents into extending their Memorial

Day campout a few more days. He hadn't had to talk much as both his parents were avid campers. On Tuesday, smoke had started to plume above the mountains to the south and news of a wild fire had reached the campground. When the boys had left the camp that morning, the sky had been clear, with the smoke plume rising high in the sky to the south of them. Two hours after reaching the ridge on which they now stood, the smoke had started to settle.

They stood and watched as planes flew in and out of the smoke, dumping slurry. From their view-point it hardly seemed to make a difference in the black rolling smoke.

"We told them where we were going," Steven said. "They won't worry."

"You don't know my mom," Jamie responded. "She worries about everything. I think we should head back"

"Well, okay, but they'll probably have that fire out pretty soon."

Jamie shook his head. He was the younger of the two, but had a wealth of common sense. "Naw, I don't think so. Maybe if the winds died, or the rains started. There's no sign of rain and the wind is going to blow. My dad said the rains aren't predicted for another few weeks. This one could be as big as the Rodeo-Chedeski Fire if they can't get it under control."

The Rodeo-Chedeski Fire in 2002 had burned 467,000 acres of forest, destroying homes, and nearly wiping out towns. It had come as far as the outskirts of Show Low, Pinetop and Lakeside just fifty miles to the west and smoke had settled in as far as Round Valley, Winslow and Holbrook. The winds had picked it up and had carried it as far as Albuquerque and up the Rio Grande Valley to northern New Mexico.

The boys turned and climbed the ridge they had just crossed. They hit the logging trail and turned down it at a fast pace. They said very little. The smoke seemed to grow thicker as they walked. Jamie was ahead about three feet, when he stopped short, looking around.

"I didn't think we had gone this far," he said. "We should have come to the road and our bikes by now. We've been walking about 30 minutes."

"We aren't lost, are we?" Steven sounded scared.

"I don't think so," the younger boy replied. "But I don't see how we could have gone so far, either. We just crossed that one ridge after we left the trail."

"It seems like we're going the wrong direction," Steven said.

Jamie frowned and looked toward the sky. "It's hard to tell with all the smoke. I can't see the sun, but it should be right about there." He raised his arm and pointed towards the spot he thought the sun should be.

"Are you sure?"

"Well, yeah. But I can't see the sun, so I don't know if it's there or not," Jamie replied. "I think we should keep going this way for another ten minutes or so, then if we don't come to the road, we'll back track and see if we can find the other trail."

"Do you think the fire will get us, Jamie?"

"Heck no," Jamie sounded more confident than he felt. "You saw where it was when we were on that ridge. It's way over there. We'll be fine. The important thing is that we stay together."

He bent to pick up a pinecone and tossed it off the road as far as he could throw it. A frown creased his brow. *'Are we lost? I'm almost certain this is the trail we followed up here, but we were just playing around. It wouldn't have taken us this long to hike back down. We must have gotten on a different log road. That has to be it.'*

Jamie didn't want to frighten Steven. Although he was the younger of the two, he had been camping with his dad a lot and knew the basic rules of survival. Steven, on the other hand, had lived in Phoenix until last year when his family had moved to the White Mountains.

He checked his watch. They had walked another ten minutes, which meant they had to retrace their steps back up the trail and try to find where they had gone wrong.

He turned.

"I think we're on the wrong trail, Steven. We're going to have to back track."

Steven looked like he was going to cry, when he pointed to the sky.

"Look! Isn't that the sun?"

Jamie looked upward. The sun, covered with layers of dark smoke was a bright red ball in the sky. And it was in the opposite direction from where he had pointed just ten minutes before.

"Yeah, that's the sun. And we are going the wrong direction. We have to hike back up the trail and find the right log road." He ducked his head and headed back up the trail. "Come on. We gotta hurry."

He heard Steven fall in behind him and he picked up his pace slightly. He wasn't scared, *yet,* but if they didn't find the trail soon, he would be. '*Mom and Dad are going to kill me,*' he thought.

They had walked about 30 minutes when Jamie stopped. "We should almost be to where we were when we started," he told Steven. "I remember we came down off the ridge and it was pretty steep, so there should be some skid marks where our feet slid down."

Steven's eyes were red and he had his hand over his nose and mouth. Jamie looked at him closely, but it didn't look as though he was crying. It was just the smoke. They continued up the trail. There ahead were the marks they had made when they slid down onto the log road. "Look," Jamie pointed excitedly. "There's where we came down off the ridge. We just have to go back to where we were and then follow our tracks back to the trail we were on to begin with."

'If we can,' he thought. *'We played around quite a while and probably walked in circles without even realizing it.'*

Jamie's eyes widened, as he looked at the slide marks they had made coming down the embankment. He didn't want to frighten Steven any more than he already was, but something else had come off that ridge since they had. He looked upward, scanning the trees around them, slowly making the circle with his eyes and his body.

"Steven, I don't want you to be scared, but I think a mountain lion came down this trail after we did."

"How do you know?" Steven asked, his voice trembling slightly.

"See, there," Jamie pointed, "That's where we slid down. The marks are fresh. And look, right there, "he outlined with his finger the track of a large animal with a padded foot.

"I'm pretty sure it's a mountain lion."

"Do you think it's after us?"

Jamie again turned slowly, looking at the trees above them. "I don't think so," he said, although he wasn't altogether sure. "I think he is probably just getting away from the smoke. Be on the lookout, just in case. Come on, we've gotta go find where we started."

The two boys climbed quickly up the embankment. At the top, Jamie looked around for their tracks. "I think we came from that way," he said pointing. "But it's so dry; we didn't leave any tracks that I can see. Let's go on to the top of the ridge and see."

Steven pointed upward, "There's one of those slurry planes and a chopper over there. I think we're almost in the right place."

"Yeah, the right place for when we were watching the planes, but not for the trail we came up on. We've got to backtrack from that ridge and see if we can find the right road. I think I kinda got turned around up here. I'm usually good with directions. At least the sun is in the right place now." The bright red-orange orb still peeped from its smoke cover. "That's weird. I hardly ever get turned around like that. My scoutmaster, Mr. Simpson, said I would be the one he would most like to be lost with, because I always had a good sense of direction. Come on. Let's see if we can find our tracks on the ridge."

"Couldn't we just keep going down the road we were on?" Steven asked. "My dad told me if I ever got lost in the woods to always follow the road down and it would eventually come to another road."

Jamie shook his head. "Naw. That's good advice your dad gave you, especially if you're lost and no one knows where you are, but we were going the wrong direction and that road could take us ten miles in the wrong direction. We need to stay in the area in case they send someone looking for us so they can find us."

Steven shrugged. "Okay, then. We'd better get going."

Chapter 5
George Doesn't Panic

Deputy George Townsend checked out at the Big Lake overflow campground at 1400 hours. There were only a few remaining campers left. He stopped at each camp, talking briefly with each camper and advising them to evacuate the area as soon as possible. Most of them were packed and ready to go. Only a few grumbled about the necessity of moving out and ruining their camping trip.

He had just about made the loop of camp spots when he saw a young man and woman hurrying towards him. They looked worried. He slowed to a stop.

The man reached him first.

"Officer, our son is missing," the man said.

"Missing, sir?"

"Yes sir," the woman said. "He and his friend left on their bikes this morning about nine o'clock and they haven't returned."

George checked his watch although he knew he'd only been in the campground a little over 20 minutes. Gone five hours. That didn't sound good.

"Do you know where they were going?" he asked.

"They said they were going to take an old logging trail up the road about three miles and see if they could see the smoke better. But they should have been back here by lunchtime."

George pulled a notebook out of his pocket.

"Your son's name, ma'am?"

"Jamie. Jamie Porter

The young man extended his hand. "I'm Bob Porter, this is my wife Camille. Let's go over to the camp table and sit down."

The three walked to the Porter's camp spot. They had a small camp trailer set up with a small tent to the side. Camille Young cleared off one end of the table and they seated themselves.

"And you say he was with a friend?"

"Yes, Steven Young. He came up here camping with us. They wanted to go look at the smoke, and I told them they could go, but they had to be back by lunchtime." Camille Porter's eyes watered up and she dashed the tears off her face. Bob Porter reached for her hand and squeezed it.

"Don't worry, sweetheart, we'll find them."

"I know."

"And you say they were only going about three miles up the road?" George asked.

"Yes," Camille said. "We noticed an old logging road up there when we were driving around the other day. The boys wanted to go explore it and I told them they could do it while we were here. Then the fire started and they decided they might be able to see the smoke better from there. You know boys."

"Yes ma'am," George grinned. "I have five of my own, so I do know." He shook his head recalling some of his own boys' antics. "And you say they left this morning about nine o'clock?"

"They were going to ride up to the log road, and stash their bikes, and then hike the rest of the way. When they didn't come back at lunch, Bob drove up to the road, but he didn't see them."

Bob added, "I drove around for a while. I did follow their tracks on the log road till it got too rocky. I don't know if they're still up there or if they came back and got their bikes and left the area."

"How old are the boys?"

"Jamie is eleven. Steven is twelve. Jamie's been out in the woods a lot. He's a smart kid. If they're lost, he'll use his head," Bob said, but George could see he wasn't sure if he really believed that when faced with the absence of his son.

"And Steven's parents? Have they been notified?"

"No," Camille said. "We didn't think, at first, there was anything to worry about. Didn't want to worry them. Jen is going to kill me." She cast a woeful look at her husband.

George stood up. "I'm going to call this in to the sheriff and get some officers up here to start a search. Meanwhile, I want you to start packing up and getting camp ready to evacuate. That fire is spreading fast and with the winds it could get worse in a matter of hours."

Bob stood by while George called the situation in to dispatch. He extracted a map from the vehicle and spread it out on the hood. Together they traced what Bob thought was the boys' route of travel.

"I didn't want to say anything while Camille was here," Bob told George, "but you know how boys are. I know they were curious about the fire. I don't think they would have tried to get to it, but they might have gone further and further so they could see it better and not realized how far they had traveled."

"That's my bet," George said. "And kids can out distance an adult in no time when they are just playing. Don't worry, Mr. Porter. We'll find those boys."

He climbed into his vehicle and rolled the window down.

"I want you and Mrs. Porter to stay close to camp so we can find you. They'll probably set up the base close by. We'll keep you apprised of anything as soon as it happens. But I also need you to get ready to pull out at a moment's notice if that fire comes any closer."

"Yes sir." Bob Porter touched the bill of his cap and turned on his heel back to his camp.

George backed his vehicle out of the campground and turned west towards the place Bob Porter thought the boys were supposed to have started their adventure. He had one more campground to visit, but it was further away from the fire and he could get it later or one of the other deputies or forest service law enforcement could cover it. His first priority was the lost boys.

"Apache-7, Apache -5,"

George reached for his mic. "Apache-7, go ahead, ma'am."

Back in Round Valley, Sheriff Andee Taylor grinned. George was always the gentleman.

"What have you got there, George?"

"Looks like a couple of kids might have gotten themselves lost while scouting out the smoke up here at the campground. One is eleven, the other twelve. They left camp around zero nine hundred this morning and were supposed to be back in camp by lunchtime. The father of one of the boys went looking just after thirteen hundred hours, with no luck.

They were just getting ready to call us when I hit the campground with the evac warning."

She checked her watch and did a quick calculation. "So they've been gone five hours or more."

"About that, ma'am."

"Is there any chance they tried to go over to the fire?"

"I guess that is always a probability where kids are concerned," George said. "But the parents don't seem to think so. Said the son is pretty woods-wise. Said he wouldn't do anything foolish."

"Okay. I've called Search and Rescue. Wade Thompson said ETA is forty-five minutes to an hour. We've got about seven more hours of daylight. I've sent Copeland up. I need as many as possible here in town. We'll regroup tomorrow if we need to."

"Ten-four. And ma'am, permission to stay on the mountain 'til they're found?"

"Okay, George. You want command?" she asked, although she already knew the answer. George wanted an active part of the search. And he'd turn over every bush and climb every tree until those boys were found.

"No ma'am. I just want to be part of the search."

"That's what I thought. Okay, George. I'll call Charlann."

"Thanks ma'am.

George Townsend checked his odometer reading when he was just past two miles and started looking for the logging road the Porters had mentioned. At just under three miles he slowed. There ahead was the road he was looking for. A huge thank-you-ma'am blocked the entrance to motor vehicles. With total disregard to the roadblock, previous vehicles had driven around the huge pile of dirt and rocks blocking the road. He knew that further up it would be impossible for anything more than a motorbike to go around, as the road became steeper with drop-offs on one side and embankment on the other.

George pulled his unit around the thank-you-ma'am and drove up the logging road about a quarter of a mile. He parked and got out. Up ahead he could see two sets of bicycle tire tracks. Taking off at a trot, he followed them up past the second thank-you-ma'am. There they veered off the logging road into a thick stand of low trees and bushes. Parting the branches, he saw two bicycles.

He backed out of the thicket and searched the ground for tracks. Two sets of footprints left the shrubbery and continued up the hill. He saw nothing to indicate the boys might have returned to retrieve their bikes.

The smoke from the fire hung thickly in the air. Long, dark pieces of soot drifted in front of his face and stuck to his clothing. He backtracked to his vehicle and pulled water and a pack from the rear cargo space. He planned to track the boys, if possible. He hoisted the pack on his back and started up the logging road, his eyes quickly darting from the boys' footprints to the area around him. He wet a kerchief and tied it around his nose and mouth to keep smoke inhalation to a minimum.

He estimated he had hiked a little over two miles up the steep mountain road, now overgrown with vegetation, when the boys' tracks veered off the road and up the embankment. The tracks had gone steadily upward until this point. George felt they had hiked with a purpose in mind; probably to get to the high ridge to the south for a better look at the smoke and the fire raging a few miles away.

He drank deeply from his bottle of water and wiped his mouth with the back of his hand. He screwed the lid back on the bottle and placed it back in its pouch. In two big steps he was up the embankment. Above the road, the terrain was rockier and harder to track. He found an overturned rock with a sneaker print, and continued on in the direction they seemed to be heading. After climbing for a quarter of a mile, he paused at the edge of a steep canyon.

"What were they thinking?" he muttered to himself. Far below a logging road stretched before him. Was it the same road he had left, or a new one? Scouting carefully around he found where the boys had stopped to rest. They had eaten a candy bar, or at least one of them had attempted to eat a candy bar. Half of it lay at the edge of a rock, half-eaten and crawling with ants. There was no paper trail. Like good scouts, they had probably put the paper into their pockets to dispose of later.

He found where they had gone off the mountain and hit the road below them, turning to walk down when they reached it. George estimated he had walked a little over five miles from his starting point when he again found tracks on the road. Two sets went down the road, and two sets went back up the road. George surmised they had gone down the road to a point and decided they were going the wrong way, then turned and went back the way they had come. He shook his head. *At least they are still together*, he thought.

He had gone a few hundred yards when another track caught his eye. On top of two of the sneaker prints were those of a mountain lion. Was the lion stalking the boys, or had he crossed their path while fleeing the fire?

George stepped up his pace and pulled his portable radio to his mouth. He eyed the large red orb that was the sun in the western sky. It had dropped considerably since he had left his vehicle. Checking his watch he figured he'd been gone a little over two hours. The sun would be behind these mountains soon, and darkness, while still a few hours away, would fall way too soon if they didn't find those boys.

He scanned the terrain ahead of him and caught his breath. More lion tracks. The big guy was not just passing through. He definitely had a plan and two young boys seemed to be the focus of it.

George keyed his mic and began walking the directions of the tracks.

Brian Copeland responded to the search and rescue call. He slowed his vehicle and turned off the main road onto the closed logging road. He spotted Townsend's unit parked about 100 yards up the trail in front of a thank-you-ma'am. He rolled to a stop beside it and called in his location.

Brian was twenty-five. He'd been a deputy for only two years, but he liked his job, most of the time. He'd grown up fascinated with cops and after some college decided to go to the police academy.

Smoke hung heavy in the air. '*This is going to kill my sinuses,*' he thought. Climbing out of his Tahoe, he raised the back and checked his pack. Pulling two bottles of water from the cooler he kept stocked for just such emergencies, he added them to his pack and hoisted it onto his back.

When he was ready to hike, he called Townsend.

"What's the ETA for Search and Rescue?" Townsend asked.

"They're setting up a base at the log road. Should be here in about 10 minutes," Brian said. "They're bringing horses."

"Good. I think we might need 'em. I've crossed their trail a couple of times. They covered a lot of ground. Not good on this old man," George tried to make light of the situation.

"There's a road to the west of the one you are on," George told him. "It's probably about a mile, maybe two. I think the boys thought it was the road they came up. They went down it a ways and retraced their steps. I think they may have gotten turned around."

Brian shrugged out of his pack and laid it across the front seat.

Townsend continued. "When rescue gets here, come up the road you're on about a mile. You'll see where the boys left the road and climbed up the mountain. I'll meet you on the second ridge about a half a mile to the west.

After a few minutes Brian heard a mic key.

"Cope?" It was Townsend.

Townsend un-keyed. There was silence. Thirty seconds passed.

"Apache 7, you there?"

"Yeah, Cope, I'm here. Listen, tell 'em not to waste time, will you?"

" Sure, what's up George?"

"Rather not say on the radio. I've notified Game and Fish. I think there might be a situation developing, and it worries me some. Just tell them to move it."

Brian tossed his pack on the front seat, started his vehicle and made a three point turn back down the road. He felt the hair on the back of his neck bristle as uneasiness pricked his senses. George Townsend was not the kind of guy who panicked easily.

He stopped at the main road and pulled across it into an empty field to wait for Search and Rescue.

Captain Wade Thompson headed up the Sheriff's Posse Search and Rescue team. After making contact with Bob and Camille Porter at the campground, he led his team of searchers west towards the logging road the boys were supposed to have taken, assuring the couple he would keep them in the loop.

Brian stepped out of his Tahoe as he saw them approaching. He spoke to Wade Thompson briefly; giving him the information George had given him. Thompson nodded.

"I've got an extra horse or two. Do you want to ride?"

Brian grinned. "It's been a while since I was on the back of a horse but, yeah, I think I'll opt for riding at this point. Sure not looking forward to hiking up that mountain."

Thompson grinned. "Going soft on us, Cope?" He motioned for the next truck to come alongside. Speaking to the driver, he gave him further instructions, then moved back into the cab of his own truck and backed it onto the flat. Killing the engine, he motioned for the next truck to do the same. Then he moved to open the tailgate of the nearest trailer and pulled down the loading ramp.

Speaking soothingly to the horses, he moved inside and untied their halters and backed each of them out of the trailer. Hoisting a blanket and saddle across the back of a sturdy dun, he cinched tight and handed a bridle to Brian. "Still remember how to do this?"

Brian took the bridle and scratched his head. "Gee, I don't know, Pop. Does this gizmo go over the ears or under the chin?" It was the easy camaraderie that goes on between men before and after a serious job. Brian bridled the horse and looped the reins around a bar on the trailer. They worked together until all four horses were saddled.

The men in the other trucks each saddled a horse and pulled out hobbles for the remaining horses.

"We'll take a mount up to George. He'll be better off searching on horseback than on foot. Can cover more ground that way."

"George said to follow this road about a mile. To the left, you'll see where the boys left the road. He tracked them up that ridge and across to another. Said it looks like they got turned around and hit another log road, but turned back. He said he'd meet us on the second ridge just above the road."

Wade Thompson looked up as Brian finished. He looked as if he was going to say something else, but closed his mouth.

"What are you nervous about Cope? Something going on you didn't tell me?"

"Not really, sir. It's just that George seemed a little agitated when I talked to him last. And, well, you know it takes a lot to shake George. He said he'd notified Game and Fish."

As if on cue, Brian's radio crackled. It was Elliott Jennings with the Wildlife Department.

"I'm five minutes away," his gruff voice relayed. "You guys go ahead. I'll catch up to you."

"Has he got a mount?" Wade asked.

"Affirmative." Elliott reported. "Saddled and ready to go."

Wade shrugged and tugged his saddle cinch tight. "Could be anything. Maybe he's got bear tracks or something."

"Could be," Brian said.

"Well, we'll soon find out." He stepped into the stirrup and mounted his horse, leading off up the hill at a brisk trot.

Chapter 6
Thursday, June 2, 2011
All P.I.S Aren't The Same

Andee stared southward. Smoke in the air was dark and heavy.

She pulled into the office parking lot and sat for a few moments, thinking. She liked being in the center of whatever was going on. Not that her deputies weren't perfectly capable of taking care of things. She knew they were. She just liked being on top of things. Waiting for word about the search was gut wrenching in itself, but waiting some 25 miles away from the action was even worse, especially now with the added danger of encroaching fire.

She shrugged and climbed out of the Tahoe. She had enough to keep her busy here in town. She might as well make the best of the job at hand.

Sandra Bradley had returned to work. Andee

greeted her as she entered the office. "How's your mom?"

Sandra smiled sadly. "She's better, but still not good. The doctor says it's only a matter of time. Could be soon or she could last for months."

"I'm sorry. I know it's got to be tough." She knew even a friendly hand on Sandra's shoulder could break the dam of tears she'd been holding back and she knew Sandra wouldn't appreciate anything that would make her break down in public.

"If you need anything… time off… anything, will you let me know?"

Sandra reached for a tissue, sniffed into it briefly, smiled a little too brightly and nodded. "Thanks Sheriff, I will." She gestured with the tissue towards the chairs along the wall that led to her office. "Uh… Sheriff, there's someone to see you…" she trailed off with an apologetic smile.

Andee turned quickly. A tall man unrolled himself from the chair where he had been slouched, legs spread. He was wearing a western cut blue chambray shirt tucked into well fitting, faded blue jeans. A small silver buckle inlaid with turquoise was attached to an inch and a half wide tooled belt threaded through the loops of his blue jeans. His boots, not new, but polished and well kept added perhaps an inch to his over six foot frame. He quickly removed the tan felt hat from his head with his left hand and stood while she approached him.

"Morgan Freeman," he said, offering his right hand to her. As tall as she was she still had to look up to meet his eyes.

"Sheriff Taylor." Andee put her own hand in his. She didn't know what she had expected. Maybe another limp-fingered squeeze that passed for a handshake? She was not prepared for the sudden weakness in her knees that she felt as he met her eyes with his own blue ones and firmly gripped and pumped her hand briefly.

"I wonder if I might have just a little of your time?" Andee glanced down at her hand still enclosed in his. She felt the heat in her face and withdrew it quickly.

"Of course." She gestured towards her office. "Would you like something to drink? We keep soda, tea or coffee in the back."

"No, I'm good for now."

Andee nodded. "If you're sure." She motioned him into her office. He stooped and retrieved a tooled leather briefcase from under the chair where he had been sitting and passed through the door into the room.

"So, Mr. Freeman. You're Bernie's friend, right? What can I do for you?" He was still standing and she realized he would remain that way until she was seated. She moved behind her desk and sat down, indicating that he too should be seated. She rested her elbows across it in front of her.

"It's Morgan. And yes I'm a friend of the *Fites*. He emphasized Fites. I was in the Marines with Jake, and attended the academy with both Jake and Sam."

"And now?" Andee knew the answer, but felt some perverse satisfaction of having him answer and seeing his reaction as she wrinkled her nose.

"Private Investigator." He tugged his wallet from his shirt pocket and flipped it open to his I.D. card. He pulled out a business card with his name emblazoned across the front and handed it to her.

She reached for it and studied it briefly.

"And, again, Mr. Freeman," she said more coolly than she had intended, strong bile rising in her throat as she thought of private investigators and sleaze-balls like Ramsey Ratliff, "What can I do for you?"

Morgan Freeman looked amused, despite her coolness.

"Well, Sheriff, I was hoping we could help each other." He leaned back in his chair and stretched lazily, revealing a taut muscular chest and slim waist beneath the thin western shirt, and worn blue jeans. He slowly pulled his length back together and sat forward in his chair.

He was all business now. His eyes hardened, his mouth tightened around the corners.

"I understand you've had a couple of reports of stolen social security numbers."

Andee answered cautiously. "A couple."

"Probably more like 5-10," Morgan smiled tightly. "Sam Fite tells me DES has been reporting to every law enforcement agency in Apache and Navajo Counties."

"Yes, but the feds are actually in charge of the investigations."

"I know. They think someone may be selling numbers to someone in Phoenix. These cases may be related."

Pulling the briefcase onto his lap, he snapped the latches open and began taking out papers and laying them one by one on top of her desk.

The first was a picture of a plain woman with short, slightly graying hair, a wide smile and vivid blue eyes.

"Melba Webster, fifty-seven. Grandmother, secretary. Disappeared a month ago from Montrose Funeral Home in Gilbert where she worked."

The next was a pretty teenager with long blonde hair and a sprinkling of freckles across her face. Her smile was full and wide and her eyes sparkled with laughter.

"Penny Dixon, seventeen , senior in high school. Disappeared three-weeks ago from Bethel Mortuary about a mile from Montrose Funeral Home.

The next picture was a slender woman with drab blonde hair. She was about thirty-five. Her smile, if anything was sad and the expression in her eyes matched it.

"Roma Montgomery. Thirty-six, married, three kids, suspected abusive husband. Worked for Rosencrans Funeral and Cremation services in Peoria. She disappeared about two weeks ago. Just before Memorial Weekend. The husband's story is that she took off on Thursday night after work with the kids to visit her mother in Apache Junction for the weekend. He said he slept most of the day on Friday and Saturday and waited for her to come home on Sunday. When she didn't show up Sunday afternoon, he called her mother. The mother said she had not seen her daughter all weekend. She said her daughter had told her that she and her husband were going to try and work a few things out with the kids out of the way. The husband said his first thought was that she had finally left him, but he called the cops anyway and filed a missing person's report.

"At first, the cops treated it as a domestic case and thought as he had said; that she had left him. But when the funeral director arrived at the funeral home on Monday morning, he found blood and signs of a struggle and called the cops."

"Wait," Andee interrupted. "He didn't go in on Friday morning? Was no one in the office of Friday? I mean, if she took off on Friday, did he just close the doors?"

Morgan shook his head. "No. He said he had a funeral director's convention to go to in Las Vegas and since Roma was going to be gone, he decided to just close the office and had his calls forwarded to his answering service."

"The blood was a match for Mrs. Montgomery's type," he continued to read from his notes. "There were no signs of breaking and entering, but two or three files had been taken from the file cabinet." He paused. "Cops figured she was taken just as she was leaving the premises. Some current files were taken from the office file cabinet."

"Melba Webster disappeared from her work place in the middle of the afternoon. The storeroom where they lock up funeral records was broken into. Several boxes of old files were taken. Melba had worked for Montrose for fifteen years. The owner, Franklin Montrose, said she was as trustworthy as a person could be. She had no family problems that he knew of. She and her husband had been married for twenty-seven years. They have a grown daughter who just had a baby. She was excited about being a grandparent. Her Dodge Geo was still in the parking lot. Her personal accounts were intact. However, two weeks ago, two of her credit cards were used in Show Low. One at Home Depot and the other at Walmart.

"And the cops think all these cases are linked?"

"They're still out on the Roma Montgomery case. The MO is a lot the same, but… they're still checking Mr. Montgomery's story."

There was a light knock on the office door and Sandra opened it briefly. "I'm sorry to interrupt," she said, "I brought you some iced tea." She set a tall tumbler on the coaster on Andee's desk. "Are you sure I can't get you something, Mr. Freeman?"

He smiled at her. "Maybe later."

"Sure, just let me know." She turned and left, closing the door firmly behind her.

Freeman picked up the photo of Penny Dixon. "Penny Dixon," he mused, as he stared at the picture. "Good kid. Not your typical teenager. A straight A-student. She has plans to become an engineer and build bridges and highways." He smiled a little wistfully. "Never gave her parents a problem. She'd been working at Bethel during the summer for three years, ever since she was a freshman. She answered phones, cleaned the funeral home, ran errands. Pinched pennies so she could pay her own tuition to college so it wouldn't put her folks out. They have two other kids and the youngest has some health problems. There's a lot of medical bills."

He paused and sat staring at the picture. "Penny was alone at the funeral home. The regular secretary, Anne Stewart, had a doctor's appointment so Penny was manning the phones while she was gone. When Anne returned Penny was gone. And the lock on the storeroom where they kept old funeral records was broken. Several boxes of files were missing."

"So what's in funeral records?" Andee asked. "Family information? Addresses? Social Security numbers?" Suddenly it clicked. "Social security numbers! They're after social security numbers!"

"More than likely. We believe someone is selling the numbers to illegals. The numbers thefts in your county could be related," he told her. "They could be completely separate, but my sources say the feds are thinking a ring of identity and social security thefts statewide.

"That's where the case is heading now," Morgan told her. "At least in Melba Webster and Penny Dixon's case. The MO is just too close to be coincidence.

"And Roma Montgomery?"

"My gut tells me there's more to the Montgomery case than identity theft. I don't know how, but I think the husband is involved in her disappearance."

"Always go with the gut," Andee said. "How do you think this office can help you Mr. Freeman?" She could not bring herself to call him Morgan. Not yet.

"Let's just say you have resources that aren't available to me off hand. And I have information that may be helpful to you in the scheme of both cases."

"I might remind you Mr. Freeman, that if you are withholding information regarding any criminal activity in this county I could arrest you for interfering in an ongoing investigation."

Morgan's eyes snapped. "You could. I hope you won't. I hope you'll trust me on this one.

"Look, I was in the county when you were getting elected. I know from the way you and your father ran your campaign that you're above petty insults and grudges. I don't have a lot of information. What I have is a little information and a big hunch. You have resources available that could, combined with what I know, help us both out."

"So I scratch your back, you scratch mine?" Andee found herself blushing at the picture that cliché brought to mind. She quickly gulped her iced tea.

Morgan grinned. "That's exactly what I'm saying, Sheriff."

"And your interest in this case, Mr. Freeman. Aren't the feds involved? Who hired you? I know that's privileged information, but what is your interest in this?"

Morgan sighed. He shuffled through the papers on her desk. Placing the photo of Penny Dixon on top, he dropped them on her desk again and tapped his finger on the photo. "Penny Dixon."

"Penny hired you? I thought she was miss--."

"Penny's my niece. She's my sister's daughter."

Andee's startled eyes met his. "Your niece?" Her expression softened. "I'm sorry. I hope you find her."

"Can we work together, Sheriff?"

Andee nodded, feeling ashamed for her earlier behavior. "I'll do what I can. I'll need copies of the information you've already gathered. Do you have a problem with that?"

"No." He pulled a bulk of papers out of his case. "This is what I've gathered to date. My sources will remain my sources for now. I'll fill you in on a need to know basis, if that's alright with you."

Andee shrugged. "For now." She gathered the papers on her desk. "Do you mind if I give these to Sandra to copy for me?" She gathered them and moved to the main room. Morgan snapped his briefcase together and locked the combination lock on it.

When Andee returned, he stood and smiled at her. "While she is copying that file, could I take you up on that offer of something to drink? I think I could go for a glass of that iced tea."

Andee smiled. "Sure. How about I show you around and we'll pick it up in the break room." She picked up her own glass. She nodded towards his briefcase. You can leave that here if you want. I'll lock up."

He dropped his case on the chair he had vacated and followed her out of the room, waiting while she pulled the door closed and checked to make sure the lock had caught.

She led the way around the oak balustrade into the hallway at the far end of the room that led to the break room in the back.

Chapter 7
Thursday
Not Afraid Of Dying

"Steven," Jamie said.

"Yeah?"

"I'm going to tell you something, and I don't want you to panic."

"What? We're lost? I think I already knew that. I dropped a candy wrapper a while back and we just walked over it again. We're going in circles, aren't we?"

Jamie grinned and poked at his friend. "Hey, you're a lot smarter than you look!" He quickly sobered.

Steven watched him carefully. "That's not it, is it?"

"Well, that's sort of one of our problems, but we've got another one, and I think it's bigger than being lost."

"We're lost and the fire is going to burn us alive?"

Steven demanded. His voice had started to tremble. "There's a stupid forest fire over there," he pointed in the direction he thought was the right way, "and no one knows where we are."

"Yes they do know," Jamie said. "And I know my mom and dad are already looking for us. The thing we gotta do is..."

"Well, I'm hungry."

"Me too, but the thing we gotta do is stop moving."

"Then how will we get outta here?"

"They'll find us. But if we keep moving, we might miss them by just five or six minutes. They'll keep going in circles looking for us, and we'll keep going in circles and we'll just miss them. That's what my scoutmaster says. So we gotta quit moving around and wait for them to find us. Only..."

He paused and turned slowly, looking upwards to the trees, and back down and around them.

"What?"

Bending over, Jamie picked up a branch about three feet long and handed it to Steven. "Hold that." Walking a little further, he found another branch and picked it up.

"What're these for?"

"Okay, Steven. Listen up. We've gotta quit moving. Sit tight, right? But remember I told you back there when we first started that a lion had stepped in our tracks?" Steven's eyes widened.

"You mean he's following us?"

"I'm not sure. But I think he is. I don't think we should take a chance."

Suddenly, as if on cue, the air was rent by a horrific snarl. Both boys jumped and stepped towards each other, seeking comfort and protection in togetherness.

"What was that?" Steven whispered, "It sounded like a woman screaming!" He stepped closer to Jamie. "Do you think someone is hurting her?"

Jamie grabbed Steven's arm and led him upward and away from the Douglas fir that grew thick against the north side of the ridge. "Come on, we've got to get up on top. Keep your stick. Don't drop it," he said as he tugged at Steven's arm.

They topped the ridge, leaving the thick fir trees behind and entering a stand of tall Ponderosa Pine. Jamie scanned the tops of each tree then let his eyes sweep over the ground before them and behind them. He fixed his eyes on a tall pine standing in a clearing and headed for it, dragging the reluctant Steven with him.

"Come on, Steve. We gotta get out of the bushes."

"What's wrong?" Steven demanded stopping and standing firmly, stubbornly.

Jamie sighed. "That wasn't a woman, Steven. I'm

pretty sure it was that mountain lion. And I'm pretty sure he wants us for his lunch. Now come on!"

He continued towards the pine tree. He didn't have to prod Steven any longer. The lowest branch on the tree he selected was about forty feet up. He approached it keeping watch all around.

When they had reached it, Jamie turned to Steven.

"Okay, this is what we gotta do. We're going to stay right here under this tree and we're going to talk to each other real loud and make a lot of noise. And we're going to stay together so that we seem a lot bigger than we really are."

"What are the branches for?" Steven asked.

"In case the lion comes at us. We'll fight him off."

"Are you crazy?"

"That's what it says to do in the books. Look big, make a lot of noise and use a stick or something to scare them with."

Steven didn't look convinced. "Are you sure it will work?'

"Sure it will," Jamie told him with false bravado. He knew it would be up to him to keep Steven talking and alert. "I read once where a little girl kept banging a stick on a tree and yelling her head off and the lion that was stalking her didn't attack. She made so much noise her folks heard her and she got rescued."

"How long has it been following us?"

"You gotta yell when you talk, Steven," he urged in a loud voice. "I don't know. Since before we went on that road, I think. Maybe before that"

"You shoulda told me."

"What?"

"You shoulda told me."

"What?"

"You shoulda told me, Jamie!" Steven screeched, his face turning red in frustration.

"There," Jamie yelled. "That's more like it." He gave Steven a reassuring boxing tap on the shoulder. "You gotta keep yelling, Steven. Make a lot of noise."

Comprehension finally sunk in as Steven realized what Jamie was doing.

"What if we lose our voices?" Steven yelled.

Jamie giggled. "Then we're lion's lunch," he yelled.

Jamie danced around the pine tree, watching the forest around them. As he came back around the tree, he held a batters stance.

"Hey, toss me a pine cone. Let's see if I can knock it outta the park."

Steven laughed.

"Yeah. Bet you can't hit nothing." He gathered up three or four large pinecones and tossed them one at a time at Jamie.

"And he swings,' he yelled with glee. "Stee-Rike

One! Told ya!"

He tossed another cone. Jamie swung, letting the weight of his 'bat' carry him around full circle.

"Stee-Rike two!" Steven yelled.

Jamie froze in his tracks. Thirty feet away, a large mountain lion crouched, watching the boys intently.

"Steven," Jamie could barely whisper.

"Hey, I thought we were supposed to be yelling. Batter, batter, batter… come on, one more strike and you're outta there."

"Steven!" This time Jamie's voice was back, along with the fear he couldn't control. "Steven, get over here! Now!"

Steven stopped his chatter and looked intently at Jamie. His eyes followed the direction Jamie had turned. He yelped, a high-pitched scream.

He crept up beside Jamie. "Wha…what do we do now?" His voice was barely above a whisper.

Jamie's mind raced while his eyes darted across the ground.

"Stay behind me and keep your stick ready. Gather up a bunch of pine cones and pile 'em up right here." He pointed beside his leg as he spoke. "Hurry. And get rocks and sticks, too if you can find any. But stay behind me and don't get too far away."

Steven needed no urging. He was glad to be doing something, even if it was wrong. He quickly gathered sticks and cones and dropped them at Jamie's feet. When he had a large pile, Jamie motioned him forward.

"Okay, now we gotta throw 'em at 'im. Did you get some rocks?"

"Yeah, a few."

"We're going to practice with pine cones first, just to see where we're hitting. If that don't scare 'im away, then we'll throw rocks. But we gotta make 'em count."

Jamie drew back and threw towards the lion. The cone landed about three feet in front of it.

Suddenly Steven came alive. He picked up several pinecones and held them loosely in the crook of his arm. "Hey batter, batter, batter…" he taunted and let fly with a cone. It hit the cougar on top of the head. The lion snarled, but held his ground.

"What's wrong, can't you hit that ole ball?" Steven yelled. He drew back and let another one fly and another right behind it. Both cones found their mark. The lion stood and snarled, then slunk back into the cover of the trees.

"I did it," Steven jumped up and down. "Did you see that? I hit him and he left."

Jamie high-fived him with a big grin. "You sure did. Wow!"

He turned quickly and started gathering more

cones, rocks and sticks. "Do you think he's coming back?" Steven asked.

"He'll be back," Jamie told him. "Those cones were just a little bother to him. Like a pesky fly. He'll be back and we gotta be ready for him."

Jamie eyed the sky. The smoke from the fire, thick and gray had allowed them to watch the sun drop behind the ridge. It would be dark soon.

The lion had returned twice and they had chased it away each time by throwing sticks, rocks and pine cones at it. But Jamie knew that in the dark, their disadvantage multiplied. He carried a waterproof container of matches in his pocket, but he hesitated to build a fire as dry as it was. They didn't need to start another forest fire. And it was hard to clear out an area while watching diligently for a lion to return. What if they fell asleep? They'd be lion's supper in no time.

"Steven?"

"Yeah?"

"You ever think about dying?"

"Not much. I used to, but I started going to church and I learned about Jesus. I don't think about it much anymore."

"How did that change you?"

"Well, I learned that Jesus loves me, and he cares for me even when I don't ask him to. He's always there as my friend, and if I die he will take me to heaven to be with him. I used to be afraid of a lot of things, but since I met Jesus, I'm not so afraid anymore."

"You met Jesus?" Jamie asked.

"Not really met him like face to face," Steven explained. "I asked Jesus into my heart. That's how I met him."

"What's that mean?"

Steven studied the ground, wrinkling his brow in thought and searching for a way to explain.

"Do you believe the Bible?"

"Yeah, I guess so. The Bible like tells you about God and all, doesn't it? It has the Ten Commandments and tells people how to live and all that."

"Yeah, that's right. But the Bible doesn't just tell you how to live; it tells you how to get a better life. It tells you how to get life forever. It is all about God's plan for us. It tells us all about the history of the world and how God created it. It tells about how God knew, even before it happened that people were going to do bad things and turn away from him. It tells us how much God loves us.

"It's kind of complicated." In the back of his mind he could hear his Sunday school teacher saying, *"When you tell others about Jesus, you must use the Bible as a reference and speak with Biblical authority."*

"John 3:16 is probably the most famous verse in

the Bible. Here, I can say it for you. It goes, 'For God so loved the world that he gave his only begotten son, that whosoever believes in Him should not perish but have everlasting life.'"

And then suddenly, he heard his mother saying, *"A witness is someone who tells what he knows. Just tell what you know."*

"God's plan is that everyone will go to heaven to be with him. But not everyone will. A lot of people don't even believe in God. They think God is just a myth."

"I believe in God," Jamie proclaimed. "I just don't know a lot about him."

Steven continued. "The New Testament is all about God's son, Jesus, and how God sent him to show the world how to live and how to have life forever.

"You mean we won't ever die?"

"Well, sort of. The Bible says that everyone has to die, but when you trust in Jesus, you become a child of God and when you die, your spirit goes to live in heaven with God and you won't ever die there."

"I thought we were all God's children."

"Not really," Steven answered "The Bible says that to become a child of God, you have to believe that Jesus is His son and ask him to live in your heart. See, God created us all, but we're not his children until we ask Jesus Christ into our heart. The Bible says that when we ask Jesus into our heart, then he becomes our personal savior. And then God adopts us and we become His children."

"How do you invite someone to live in your heart? That sounds weird."

"Well, it means that you gotta believe that Jesus is God's son and that he died on the cross to take away the bad things you do. The Bible says that everyone does bad things. We're born with the desire to be bad. But when we recognize that and we are sorry for it, then we gotta ask God to forgive us. When we do that and tell God that we believe in Jesus, then he forgives us and we become his children. Then when we die, we go to heaven to be with him. But even better than that, he comes to live in our heart and he never leaves us."

"How can someone live in your heart?"

"I'm not sure. I just know he does. It's because God is a Spirit and a spirit can live anywhere, even in your heart. And then when I'm afraid, or sad or lonely, He is there to make it better."

"Have you done it? Asked God to forgive you and let you be one of his children?"

"Yep. Last summer at Vacation Bible School. Then I got baptized, too."

Jamie was quiet. His parents didn't go to church

very often. His dad liked to fish and camp so most of their weekends were spent in the mountains. And when they did go to church, the priest didn't mention anything about personal saviors.

"So, what did you do?" he finally asked. "To get Jesus as your personal savior?"

"I just told him I was sorry for all the things I done wrong. And I asked him to forgive me for all of them, even the ones I couldn't remember. I told him that I believed that Jesus Christ was his son, and that he died for me, and that I wanted him to be my savior and live in my heart forever."

"You talked to God like that?"

"My Bible teacher says you don't have to pray all pretty or nothing. You just tell God what's in your heart. You don't even have to pray out loud, but I did. And I always pray out loud at night, so I won't go to sleep before my prayers are finished."

"Steven?"

"Yeah?"

"So, you aren't afraid to die?"

Steven shrugged. "I guess I'm not really afraid to die. I know when I die God will take me to heaven to live with him forever. But I'm scared of that lion out there. And I guess I'm scared that if he decides to eat us, it'll hurt. I'm scared of that. But I'm not really scared of dying."

"Does having Jesus for your personal savior do that? Make you not afraid to die?"

"Yeah, I guess it does. Cuz I used to have bad dreams about it all the time. But now, since I got him for my savior, and he lives in my heart," Steven shrugged, "not so much anymore."

"Can I get him for my savior?"

Steven's eyes widened. His thoughts whirled. His Sunday school teacher had told him that when he became a Christian it was his duty to tell others about Jesus, but he never had. Sometimes he felt guilty about it, but it was so hard to bring up the subject. But this wasn't hard at all. Jamie had just asked him questions and he had answered them.

"Sure," he grinned from ear to ear. "You just gotta do like I said. You tell God you're sorry for all the bad things you done, even the ones you don't remember, and ask him to forgive you for them. Then just ask Jesus to come into your heart. That's all there is to it."

"I'm not sure I know how to pray. I'm afraid to close my eyes. Don't you gotta close your eyes when you pray?"

"Heck no," Steven shouted, pounding Jamie on the back. "Do you shut your eyes when you talk to your dad?"

"No-o-o."

"Well, then… you don't hafta shut your eyes when

you talk to God neither. You just talk to him. Here, I'll help you. But you gotta really mean it."

"I do. I want Jesus in my heart like you have him."

"Okay, just say, 'Oh God. I love you.'" He waited for Jamie to repeat his words. "Then tell him you love Jesus too. Okay, now tell him you're sorry for all the bad things you done. And ask him to forgive you. Now tell him you want Jesus to be your savior."

Jamie finished his prayer and blinked quickly as tears sprang to his eyes. He turned away from Steven feigning a watchful eye into the woods, even as he dashed the moisture from his eyes.

Steven slapped his back again. "Don't be embarrassed. I cried a little when I got saved too. My mom said that is just Jesus cleaning up our insides with water and some of it spills over. My dad says that real men know how and when to cry and there is nothing wrong with it as long as you don't get wimpy." He giggled. "Idn't funny how we're told when we're little not to cry 'cause we're big boys, then we get saved and it's manly to cry." He shook his head and grinned. "Adults. Can't make up their minds."

By then Jamie had recovered.

"So now if I die, I'll go to heaven?"

"Yep. But we aren't going to die tonight. They'll find us." Suddenly he had become the strong one. "I bet they'll be here in less than an hour."

Chapter 8
Thursday

A Body On The Mountain

The crew on Engine 62 had been working steadily through the night and into the next day with just quick snatches of rest. They'd pulled back twice when the fire had jumped fire lines. The winds had not abated and the fire fanned bigger with every passing moment. Spot fires, embers pushed by the wind from the main fire were being dropped as far as five miles ahead of the fire. Only four days since it had started and it had already burned almost 7,000 acres. They were hoping to find a ridge in front of the fire for crews to begin a new line.

"I know we passed a logging road when we were on patrol last week." Steve Connors told his crewmates. "And I think it's still open. It was just after we stopped for that Roger Smith guy last week."

"You're right," Gwen Watson agreed with him. "I remember seeing it too. It's pretty rough, but I'll bet it will take us right up on that ridge we were looking at." They noted the sheriff's vehicles and search and rescue trucks and trailers parked beside the road. John Wilson pulled to a stop. A deputy waved at him and walked to the truck. He explained to the engine crew about the hunt for the two boys.

John thanked the deputy and told him they'd keep their eyes open, before shoving the truck into gear and continuing up the grade.

"Here's where our Mr. Smith was," John said as they passed the spot where they had stopped earlier.

"That was one weird man," Steve commented.

Wendy Thompson shuddered. "He gave me the creeps. Did you see how he looked at Gwen and me?"

"Everyone looks at you, Wendy," Tom Sly told her laughingly. And it was true. Wendy was a pretty girl and men, especially, looked at her longer than most.

Wendy smacked Tom on the shoulder, playfully. "He looked at me differently than creeps like you look at me," she told him. "He looked at me like I was some kind of bug he wanted to squish."

"Yeah," Gwen said. "I noticed that, too. It was creepy."

"Besides, that," Wendy continued. "I don't think

he was up here to do any fishing."

"What makes you say that," John Wilson asked.

"Did you see any fishing gear? I didn't. I looked in the back of that Jeep Cherokee he was driving. And those clothes he was wearing. Did they say fisherman to you?" She shook her head emphatically from side to side. "Huh uh, I don't think so. That guy wasn't fishing."

"And when you asked him his name, it was like he had to think about it," Wendy continued. "I'll bet his name isn't Roger Smith at all."

"He seemed mighty jumpy and nervous to me," Gwen said. "He was just weird. Did you notice what rental company that jeep was from?"

"It was Hudson's, from over in Show Low, but I think the main office is in Phoenix," Steve Connors supplied. "I recognized the emblem on the back window. I rented a car from them once."

John drove for another two miles before finding the road he was seeking. Just as he had remembered, it was still open to vehicular traffic. He made a sharp left turn and plunged the truck onto its narrow and rutted track. "Hold on to your hats," he cautioned, "this ain't no freeway."

The road twisted and turned around the side of the mountain, climbing upward, sometimes gradually, sometimes steeply. They had traveled approximately three miles when the road leveled off and they rounded a curve. John braked and pulled the engine to a full stop.

"Looks like this is as far as we go boys."

Two large boulders had fallen into the road from the cut above them. "Unless you guys think you can move those rocks, we're stuck."

The crew piled out securing neckerchiefs to their faces to block out as much smoke as possible and began to tug and pull at the rocks, inching them across the road and to the edge of the embankment. With the two largest ones off to the side, they began picking up the smaller ones and carrying them to the ditch on the embankment side.

When they were down to a dozen or so, Gwen tugged at Wendy's coat and nodded her head indicating the road they had just traveled. "Nature call," she said. "I don't think I can make it much further over this rough road."

The women headed down the road then turned off it into a thick stand of fir trees.

Wendy wrinkled her nose, "Eww, what's that smell?" she asked.

"Well, it's not me," Gwen laughed, then sobered. "It is kind of rank, isn't it? Smells like something dead."

From their hiding place amidst the trees they

could hear a buzzing. "Whew," Wendy gasped, fanning her hand in front of her face. Even with the kerchief over her face, the smell gagged her. "I'm not so sure choosing this direction was such a good idea. That is the worst smell I ever smelled. Ugh."

Gwen nodded assent. "Yeah, I don't like it. Check on the guys. I think we need to find where the smell is coming from."

"Are you kidding? I don't want to get any closer than we already are. That is awful."

"I know," Gwen agreed. "But I don't think it's a dead animal, Wendy. I've been around animals. This smells more like human decomp."

When Gwen wasn't fighting fire she worked with the Search & Rescue Specialty Unit that specialized in retrieving victims from plane crashes, car wrecks off canyon walls and lost hikers who had fallen. Too often bodies began to decompose before they were found and the team could get to them. She knew the smell of decomposing human was different from animal decomp. There was a sickly sweetness in human decomp and she was pretty sure that was what they were smelling.

Wendy's mouth dropped. "No. You mean like a dead person? No! You're kidding, Gwen! Please tell me you're kidding."

"I wish I were, Wen. Go check on the guys and

I'll look for the source."

Wendy headed back to the road, looking back over her shoulder. "You're sure you want to do this?"

Gwen shrugged. "Not what I want. What we have to do, Wen. Now go. Get the guys."

Gwen returned to the road and walked back and forth on the hard surface, watching the shallow bar ditch that allowed water to run down the side of the road to a ditch about twenty yards below. She moved back towards the truck and lost some of the smell. She retraced her steps and continued past the tracks up the embankment that she and Wendy had left. She'd only gone about ten more yards when she found more tracks going up the embankment. Looking up the hill she could see a brush pile left from a former logging operation. She skirted the scarred embankment, being careful that she didn't disturb the tracks. Circling the brush pile, she approached from above it. She didn't want to get too close and risk disturbing any evidence, if this was a human corpse.

When she was within twenty feet of the brush pile, she could see and hear huge green blowflies buzzing and rising in and out of the debris. She approached cautiously, watching for tracks. She saw none in the soft ground above the brush pile. Drawing closer, she covered her mouth and nose with her sleeve. Peering under the reddened pine needles and branches she caught sight of black plastic. Moving closer, she realized it was a heavy duty black body bag used to transport worst-case victims of accidents, shootings, stabbings or animal maulings.

She retraced her steps and had just made it back to the road when she heard the rest of the crew coming down. She hastened ahead to meet them. One look at her grim face told them the news wasn't good.

"We need to call the sheriff's office," she told them. "I'm pretty sure we have human remains in a bag up there."

They turned and headed back towards the engine.

"You're sure?" Tom Sly asked.

"As sure as I can be from the smell and without messing up the scene. There is a black body bag in a pile of brush up there. I can't see anyone putting an animal in a hundred dollar body bag and dumping it."

They reached the truck. John opened the door and reached for the mic. "You know the details, you'd better call it in," he told Gwen, handing her the mic. She thanked him and took the mic, keying it to call her dispatcher.

When she was through, she hung the mic on the peg and turned to her peers. "Sheriff's deputies are already in the area looking for those lost boys. They'll have someone up here in a little while."

She opened the back door and hauled out a small, insulated ice chest. Taking a bottle of water from inside, she unscrewed the lid and took a long swig. "I'm hungry. Was there any of that chicken left?"

Wendy's mouth dropped open. "You're hungry? After smelling that foul odor? You've got to be kidding. How can you eat with that smell still in your nostrils?"

Gwen grinned at her. "Best way to get rid of a putrid smell is to eat something good. It replaces the bad with the good." She dug into another insulated chest and removed a drumstick. Winking at the men, she bit a hunk out of it and began to chew. "Anyone else?" When they all shuddered and refused, she laughed. "I'm sorry guys. When I'm nervous, I eat. And this makes me nervous." She walked to the side of the road and plopped down on a rock and leaned back against the embankment on the side of the road.

"Are there any more obstructions up the road like this one?"

"Not as far as we walked," John answered her. "If it's not any worse than this, we can handle it, I think. Provided we don't get held up here for long."

Gwen nodded. "They'll just want preliminary answers for now. They know where to find us if they need anything further. We should probably meet them down below where the tracks are. If there are any tire tracks besides ours they won't be able to distinguish if more vehicles come up the road." She hitched herself off the rock and began walking back down the road.

They didn't have to wait long for the deputies. They heard the labor of an engine long before they saw the white Chevy Tahoe round curve.

Deputy Ren Dew, lowered his window, then opened his door and stepped out to meet the six young people on the road before him. He recognized Gwen Watson and John Wilson. Gwen stepped forward with a grim look on her face. "Hi, Ren."

Ren touched his hat to her and nodded to the other five. "What's up?"

"Take a deep whiff," Gwen told him. "We were headed up to the ridge and had to move some rocks from the road. Wendy and I took a nature call," she pointed ahead up the hill, "and encountered a decomp smell. I'm pretty sure we have human decomp in the bushes up there."

Ren walked to the back of his rig and unlocked the door. He pulled out yellow plastic marking tape, rubber gloves and work gloves. "Okay," he said. "Wanna show me?"

Gwen turned and Ren fell into step beside her. The other five followed behind. She moved to the outer edges of the road and the others followed. "I'm not sure if there are tracks or evidence on the road here, so after I found …it, we tried not to disturb anything further."

She turned up the hill before reaching the site. The rest of the crew stayed behind on the road. Ren followed her up the hill. "I approached from above. If someone dumped the body, if it is a body, I figure they'd have gone from the road straight up."

They came to the pile of brush with the telltale flies buzzing around it.

"Sure smells human," Ren agreed with her. "Well, help me secure the area to start, and then I'll call the sheriff." He handed Gwen the roll of yellow plastic tape and pointed to a pine tree about 100 feet behind them. "Attach the end to that tree. We'll swing wide to encompass our tracks down to the road and around and back up to this tree. Did you notice any vehicle tracks on the road?"

Gwen nodded. "Yeah. They're faint though. This wind has blown sand in them. There are tracks from the road leading up the hill towards this brush pile." She handed the tape back to Ren and headed down the hill the way they had come up.

Arriving back at his vehicle, he called dispatch and was patched through to the sheriff.

"What have you got, Ren" Andee asked.

"Pretty sure we've got a DB up here near the

search site," Ren told her. It's on the road about two miles west of the road those boys took up the mountain. A fire engine crew stopped to clear some rocks and smelled it and called it in."

Andee frowned. This was starting to be a nightmare week. "Okay, Ren, I'll meet you up there in about an hour and a half. Secure the scene and get a report from the fire crew."

"Yes ma'am."

Ren took the tape from Gwen and continued to tie off around the scene. He returned to his truck and motioned for the fire crew to gather round.

"Look, I know you guys have a job to do and I'll not keep you from it." He looked at Gwen. "You said you stopped to move rocks?"

She nodded. "More like boulders." She pointed toward the rocky point above the road where they had parked. "We couldn't get around them in the engine, so we stopped to see if we could shove them off. We managed to get most of them, and Wendy and I decided to take a nature call. The guys went around the bend to see if the road was clear. We smelled decomp and I sent Wendy back to tell the guys. I circled from the road around and came down on that brush pile. Before I got too close, I could see a black plastic bag. It looked like one of those heavy duty body bags we use for our worst cases on our S & R."

"And you didn't get any nearer than what you showed me?"

"No."

"What's your phone number, Gwen?"

She told him and he quickly jotted it down and got the names and numbers of the rest of the crew.

"Someone will be in touch. You guys go on and fight fire. Be safe." He shook hands with them all and they headed up the trail toward their engine.

Chapter 9
Thursday
Why The Sheriff?

Andee hung up the phone and turned to Morgan Freeman. "You want to take a trip up the mountain? We've got a possible body dump up there and I've got one of those gut feelings."

Morgan gulped down the rest of his iced tea and set his glass on the counter in the break room. "I'm ready when you are."

Andee retraced their steps to the front office.

"Sandy, we've got a possible body dump up near the search site for those lost boys. Call Carlie. Tell her to meet me there and call in a couple of the off duties. Whoever is on-call. Tell them I need some more town coverage. Then call Bernie and tell her to hold the fort till I get back. I'm headed up the mountain to that search site."

Sandra grimaced and turned to the phone on her desk. "Will do. Oh, and I've got those copies you wanted, Sheriff." She indicated a stack of papers on the corner of her desk.

Andee picked them up and carried them through to her office with Morgan following closely.

"I just need to put these in a folder and lock up," she told him. "Do you want to take your case or leave it here?"

"I'll take it," Morgan told her. "I might need it."

She shrugged and deposited her documents in her file cabinet and locked it up. She handed Morgan his copies and stood by while he stored them in his briefcase.

"Do you have a jacket? It gets cold up on the mountain once the sun sets."

Morgan grinned. "Yeah, I know. There's one in my truck. I'll get it on the way out."

Andee locked up and waved to Sandra. "Call me if you need me."

Andee pushed a button on the automatic locking device on her key ring. Her Tahoe chirped instead of opening. She realized she'd hit the wrong button. Fumbling to make sure to hit the right one, she double clicked it and heard the locks on all her doors snap open.

She stepped up on the running board and hoisted

herself into the driver's seat. After turning the key in the ignition she turned the volume down on the CD player and adjusted it on her two-way, while she waited for Morgan Freeman to join her.

She would rather have been taking this call alone, but in view of what he had just told her, she felt it only fair to include him, just in case this turned out to be one of the missing women he was searching for.

He opened the back door and tossed his jacket and briefcase onto the back seat, then joined her in the front. After buckling in, he turned and grinned sheepishly. "I probably should have stayed a cop and joined one of the forces up here in the mountains. I still get a rush when there's a call."

Andee responded before she could think. "I don't think it ever goes away. My Uncle Douglas retired from the police force up in Portland. He says he still gets the urge to respond when he hears a siren. Aunt Molly finally made him take his scanner out to the garage so she didn't have to listen to it all the time. Which served two purposes," she laughed and turned right onto Mountain Avenue. "It got him out of the house, too."

Morgan chuckled. "How did she feel about him being a cop?"

"Very supportive. She worked as Emergency and 911-dispatcher for years. She actually wanted to be a cop, but she's only five feet tall and weighs about ninety pounds. That's probably below requirements, even today, but back in the day, even if she had been two hundred pounds and six foot seven, there was no way she would have been accepted into the academy. So she settled for dispatcher, a woman's job, you know? It kept her in the circle."

"So, why did you become a cop?" Morgan asked her.

Andee blushed and looked out her side window, briefly. "All the usual reasons, I guess; to do something for the community, for mankind; to make a difference."

"Why not a school teacher or a nurse?"

"Do you have something against women becoming cops?" she asked quickly, defensively.

"Not at all. Some of the best cops I know are women. You just don't seem…I mean, you're different. You're not like other women cops I know."

"Different? Really? In what way?"

He shrugged. "Keep your hands on the wheel, and don't hit me. But you seem softer. Not as hard around the edges. I would have figured you more for a school teacher."

Andee laughed. "My mom is a school teacher. And a Sunday school teacher. She loves kids. And when I was little, I wanted to be just like my mom.

But as I got older, I realized kids, little kids, as a whole, scare me to death. Kids? War Zone, Cop? Piece of cake.

"You don't like kids?" She thought he sounded disappointed, but that was silly. Why would he be?

"No, I love kids. I love my sister's kids. I love my cousin's kids. I like kids in general. It's just as a whole, in mass. They scare me to death." She giggled. "I don't know how my mom does it. She takes care of bloody noses, picks splinters, consoles little girls who have broken hearts when puppy love doesn't work out and she makes peace among boys who are fighting. They all love her." She beamed, thinking of her mother. "She's a wonder."

"So a room full of kids scares you worse than facing some idiot kid high on meth or a crazed man with a loaded gun?"

"You betcha! At least I know the unknowns in cases like that. Anything could happen, so you prepare for the worst. With a room full of kids, it could be peaceful and quiet one moment and a total uncontrollable riot the next. No thanks!"

Morgan laughed. "I guess that's one way of looking at it. So why the sheriff? Why not just a street cop or just a deputy?"

"I'm not sure. It's not like I went to the academy so I could become the sheriff. I applied to several departments before I decided to run for sheriff. To tell you the truth, no one was more surprised than me when I won the election."

"Really? Why's that?"

She shrugged. "Lack of experience, age, gender, a lot of things. I really didn't think I had the chance of a snowball in hell."

"Now come on. You against Hilton Parks? No contest."

"Why?" She was serious. "Parks had been sheriff for twenty years. Most of the county thought he was doing a good job."

"Not in my neck of the woods. Not everything you heard on the rumor mill was rumor, you know? My neighbors would have voted for you if… I mean, they were looking for a change. They would have voted for anyone."

Andee felt her hackles rise. She gripped the steering wheel and looked straight ahead. Through clenched teeth she said, "Just exactly what does that mean? You don't think I'm qualified for the job?"

"No, I mean yes, you're qualified. Don't fly off the handle and get all female on me. That came out wrong. What I meant was, Parks was a crook. It was time for an honest candidate. Even if you hadn't been qualified, your honesty, the clean way you ran your campaign, it all amounted to a huge landslide for you.

I even…." He trailed off.

"What? You even what?"

"I even thought you were the best candidate," he grinned. "Bar none."

"Yeah right."

"Why don't you like me?"

"What?" she seemed to be using that word to question everything he said. "What makes you think I don't like you? I don't even know you."

"But you don't, do you?"

"I don't know you," she said firmly. "I'm reserving judgment."

"Sure you are."

Andee made a left off SR260 onto SR273 and then on FR68. The road began immediately to wind upward. Andee concentrated on her driving, taking the curves at about ten miles faster than posted.

Morgan sat silently beside her, seemingly unperturbed by her driving. Not once did he clutch the armrest nor did she feel him tense up.

He mentally kicked himself. He needed her cooperation on this case. He had a bad feeling about what they were going to find on the mountain. He prayed that if it really was a human body the fire fighters had found that it wouldn't turn out to be Penny.

Chapter 10
Thursday

The Rescue

Elliott Jennings caught up to Brian Copeland and Wade Thompson as they led the search and rescue team up the mountain. They reached the appointed ridge and found George Townsend waiting for them.

"I'm pretty sure we've got a cougar in the area, and it's crossed tracks with the boys a couple of times," George told them. "If he's stalking those kids, they won't have a chance after dark." He pointed out where he'd found tracks. "I'm going back up to where I lost their tracks, about an eighth of a mile north." He pointed southward. "That other logging road runs down there, but when it starts climbing out, it gets pretty steep. I don't think they would have taken it, but we can't chance it. You're in charge Wade, but

I think I'd send a couple of men over to that trail to scout for tracks, and maybe the rest of us fan out to the south. I've got a hunch they are going in circles, but they're south of the road."

"Sounds like a plan," Wade grinned. "Grady, you and Lee head south to that logging road. Try and pick up the trail where they got on the road or left it. If you don't find anything soon, move up the ridge towards the south and meet us before dark."

Grady and Lee turned their horses southward. Wade clucked to his mount, nudged his side and joined Townsend as they moved up the hill.

They reached the top of a small rise within the mountain. "This is where I lost both tracks," George told the group.

They dismounted and spread out, watching the ground closely.

Brian bent and picked up a piece of candy wrapper. Then a little further away, the impression of a canvas shoe. "I think I've found the trail," he said. Wade confirmed and the men mounted. They spread out, calling out the boys' names periodically. After an hour they lost the trail again and dismounted to search on foot.

Suddenly Brian's horse snorted and tossed his head, backing away.

"Whoa, boy." Brian tightened his grip on the reins

and reached to calm his mount. The horse snorted again and tossed his head. "Easy boy."

The sudden, piercing scream of a cougar rent the air. The men held tight to their mounts, trying to calm them.

"Which direction did that come from?" Brian asked. Wade and George both pointed towards the southwest, while one of the other men pointed due west. "Brian mounted and nudged his horse to follow George and Wade, who were already leading out at a brisk pace.

"Ste--ven! Ja--mie! Ste--ven! Ja--mie!" The men continued to call as they moved.

"Did ya hear that?" Steven yelled. "Did ya hear that Jamie? I heard someone calling us?"

"Shhh." Jamie held up his hand. "It might be the wind."

They listened a full minute before hearing a man's voice distinctly calling, "Ste--ven! Jam--ie!"

Jamie yelped and jumped in the air. "Whee-oo! Over here!" He began jumping up and down. "Over here! We're over here." He grinned at Steven. "They found us. They found us. Yell! Yell! Hey, hey, we're over here."

Steven joined in his shouts. Five minutes later they heard the ring of shoed horses on the rocks and the jingle of bridle. "We're here!" Jamie cried. "Over here! Right in front of you."

The search and rescue team rode into sight. The boys sobered and looked at each other. They high-fived then ran towards their rescuers. Words tumbled over excited words and they embraced the men who had found them.

George Townsend turned to dig in his pack and offered water to each boy. "You boys really gave us a scare." He tried to sound gruff.

"I guess we got turned around," Jamie told him sheepishly. "We're really sorry. I've never been lost before. I tried to remember what my dad told me, but then that ole lion started screaming at us, and then we saw it. I guess I just kind of lost track of all those lessons."

"Naw, you didn't," Steven admonished. "You said we were probably going in circles, and made us stop. And you knew how to keep that lion from eating us for dinner."

"Yeah, I think you done good, boys," George conceded. He nodded at Elliott

"This here's Elliott Jennings," he told them. "He's with the Game and Wildlife Department. You boys need to talk to him a few minutes about this lion. Did you see actually see him?"

Steven and Jamie nodded, wide eyed. Elliott dismounted. Placing a hand on the shoulder of each boy, he asked, "You saw him? You're sure it was a cougar, a mountain lion?"

Jamie nodded vigorously and Steven agreed. "He was just over there by those trees," he pointed. "We gathered pine cones and rocks and stuff and threw them at him." Steven beamed. "I hit him on the head with a rock and he moved back into the trees."

Elliott smiled. "That was pretty good pitching. How long ago was that?"

Jamie shrugged. "Maybe 15 minutes before you guys found us. Steven hit him and he moved back into the trees. Then he let out this fierce scream like he was really mad or something. Then a little while later we heard you guys calling our names."

He looked around nervously. "Do you think he's still around?"

"Well, I'm going to have a little look-see and find out," Elliott told them. "You boys go ahead with these guys, okay?"

Elliott turned to Wade Thompson. "Any of your guys want to tag along?"

Wade turned to look over his men. Jim Turley and Fox Bennet kicked their horses forward. "We'll stay."

"Are you ready to get down the mountain?" George asked the boys. "Your folks are worried and it's going to be dark soon."

"You bet." Jamie told him. "Can we ride the horses?"

"Sure thing." George lifted him up and put him behind Brian. "This here's Deputy Brian Copeland. He's been riding horses since he was about your size. Just hold on tight. It's pretty rough going back to the road."

"Yes sir." Jamie fastened his arms around Brian's waist.

George turned to Steven. "You ready?"

Steven swallowed nervously and nodded.

"Have you ever ridden a horse before?"

"No."

"Nothing to it," George assured him. "This here is Wade Thompson. He's the head of Valley Search and Rescue. You just hold on to him tight." He lifted Steven up behind Wade. "Just put your arms around his waist and hold on. He won't let you fall." He patted Steven's leg. "How's that? You gonna be alright?"

"Yes sir. I think so."

"Okay. Let's move out."

He mounted his horse and clicked the mic on his epaulet.

"Dispatch- Apache-7. We've found the boys. We're Code-4. We're headed off the mountain."

"Ten-four, 2033 hours sir." They had been searching for almost six hours.

Chapter 11
Thursday
I Left A Message

The young girl practically squealed with delight, then covered her mouth with her hand and smiled at the older woman standing beside her.

"We did it! I think I can get through there."

The older woman nodded. "I think so. Come on. You need to leave now before they come back."

She motioned for the young girl to step up on the chair that was beneath the small window overhead. "Come on, now. You must hurry."

The young girl threw her arms around the older woman. Tears filled her eyes. "I'll bring help, Melba, I promise."

"I know you will. Just be careful."

Penny quickly climbed up on the chair and lifted the window. Melba cupped her hands and the young girl put her foot into the cup. With a gentle boost, she slithered through the window. She was free. "There's a fire somewhere," she called back through the window. "It's really smoky out here. I'll be back as soon as I can," she whispered.

"Just send the police, Penny. Don't come back. Don't worry about me. Just send the police."

"I will." She lowered the window and turned to survey her surroundings. It was almost dark, but she could make out the outline of several buildings around her. She'd just escaped from the basement of a rather old decrepit looking house. There were no lights on the lower floors. The setting sun left a slight glow to the west and Penny quickly got her bearings.

To the west she could see the lights of a town. It wasn't a large town. She knew her kidnappers had driven for about 4 hours before finally stopping. She'd been moved twice before being put in the basement of the old house with Melba Webster. She could be anywhere within a four state region, but she thought she was still in Arizona. She hoped she was.

Looking about cautiously she found the driveway and headed towards the road that lead into town. There was quite a lot of brush and undergrowth as well as trees and she kept to the side of the road in case she had to hide.

It took almost an hour to reach the town. The

road she was on turned into a black topped highway at the edge of town. Again she looked around to get her bearings. To her left, about a half a mile away she saw the lights of a house, but the main section of town seemed closer. She struck out anxious to find a phone or some human contact. Ahead she caught a glimpse of a gas station and hurried her steps. Just as she rounded the corner, a sheriff's vehicle pulled onto the concrete pad in front of the store and a tall, lanky deputy crawled out of the front seat.

Suddenly Penny remembered a conversation she'd distinctly heard shortly after being imprisoned in the basement of the old house. She pulled back into the shadows and waited for the man to enter the store. As much as she wanted to trust the local police, one of her captors had called the other one, who seemed to be the boss, Sheriff. She could not take any chances. A phone booth was attached to the front of the store. She quickly dug into her jeans pocket and pulled out two quarters. She dialed a number and turned her back on the officer exiting the store with a paper sack in his hand. The odor from the sack reminded her that she had not eaten since breakfast.

The phone rang for the sixth time as the deputy backed off the cement pad and drove into the street. The line went to the answering machine.

"Uncle Morgan," Penny spoke quickly. "It's

Penny. I'm okay. I'm with a woman named Melba Webster. They are holding us in the basement of an old house about three miles east of St. Johns. Or at least I think it is St. Johns. I got out through a small window, but I'm going back to be with Melba. I don't know what they will do to her if they find I'm gone. Uncle Morgan, I think the sheriff is involved. Don't trust the sheriff. Please come get me Uncle Morgan. Tell mom and dad I am okay and I love them."

Another vehicle pulled into the lot behind Penny. She glanced over her shoulder. Another sheriff's vehicle. "Please hurry," she whispered into the phone and hung up. She kept her back turned until the deputy entered the store, and then retreated to the rear of the building.

She waited until the deputy left. Digging in her pocket she counted a little over ten dollars in coin and bills. She turned and entered the store. A warming oven covered half the front counter. She asked the price of the burritos resting under the glass and ordered four of them. She paid the clerk her money and left the store.

The wind had died. Walking back to the farm went faster than the trip into town, but the smoke made breathing hard. She approached the farm house with caution. It still looked abandoned. She cautiously made her way across the yard and ducked down near the basement window. Tapping lightly, she waited for Melba to unlatch the window. When it was open, Melba peered out.

She opened the window. "Oh, Penny, what are you doing back here? Why didn't you stay away? Oh, I wanted you to stay away. There is no telling what they will do to us when they come back."

Penny slithered through the open window, and fastened the window again. "Here," she offered the sack of food. "I brought us something to eat."

"But why did you come back child? You were safe. Oh you should have stayed away." Penny grinned impishly. If Melba had not been holding the sack of burritos, she would have been wringing her hands.

"I couldn't leave you here alone. I think there is a big fire somewhere. There is heavy smoke settling in," she told Melba. "Besides, if they came back and found me gone, they might kill you. This way they will never know I left. I called my Uncle Morgan. He lives in Vernon. I think that is south of where we are right now. He'll come for us."

"Did you talk to him? Is he coming, really? Where are we?" Questions seemed to fly from Melba's mouth as fast as her brain could form them.

"No, I didn't talk to him, exactly. But I left a message on his machine. As soon as he gets it he will come get us. I think we are just outside St. Johns. I've heard Daddy and Uncle Morgan talk about it. It's about thirty miles south of Round Valley."

"But didn't you say your uncle was a private investigator? What if he is away on a case? What if he doesn't get it until too late?"

"Where's that positive attitude you were telling me to keep?" Penny scolded. "Listen, they haven't harmed us yet. I think the only reason they took us was because we were in the way and it was the fastest way to get out of town with those records. If they had wanted to hurt us, they would have done it already. How many times have they moved us? Wouldn't it have been easier to just kill us and dump us into a canyon somewhere? The reason I came back is because I don't want to rock the boat. Besides they haven't fed us since morning, and I knew you were as hungry as I am. So let's eat and figure out how we are going to get out of here if Uncle Morgan doesn't come for us soon."

Chapter 12
Thursday night
Just A Bit Of Evidence

It was dusk by the time Andee and Morgan reached the search base. The smoke from the fire was thick. The sky glowed orange and gold to the south. She pulled in beside a horse trailer just as the deputies were crossing the clearing on their horses. Brian Copeland waved and shouted.

Andee climbed out of her Tahoe and greeted him. "Parents are on the way." Morgan came up beside her and reached for the boy behind Brian.

"Hey, son. I hear you've had quite an adventure today."

Jamie grinned sheepishly. "Yes, sir. We almost got eaten by a big ole cougar."

"That's what I heard. I'm glad you boys are okay."

He moved to the other horse and lifted Steven

from behind the saddle.

"Reckon you'll have a great story to tell your friends when you get back."

"Yes, sir. But they'll never believe it."

A vehicle pulled in behind Andee's Tahoe, dust flying. Camille Porter was out of the car before it had completely stopped. "Jamie!" she screamed as she practically knocked him off his feet in a huge embrace. Tears streamed down her cheeks.

"Mom." Jamie struggled out of his mom's embrace, and looked sheepishly at his dad. "Mom, we're fine. I'm sorry. We didn't mean to get lost. We got turned around, and then that ole cougar started following us…"

"What? A cougar? Oh my gosh, Jamie. Oh my gosh." She stepped towards him as if to hug him again, but he stepped back.

"Really, Mom, we're okay."

Bob Porter looked at Brian.

"There was a cougar?"

Brian nodded. "There was. But I have to tell you, Mr. Porter, your son handled the situation like a pro. He said you'd taught him how to survive in the woods. You did a good job, sir. He did all the right things once he realized they were going in circles and being hunted. They stopped and took up a defensive position."

Wade Thompson stepped forward and shook Porter's hand. "I hate to cut this reunion short, sir, but that fire is edging closer and closer. We need you to get your family down the mountain to safety. We've got another call to take care of up here, then we'll be clearing out as well. The smoke is pretty heavy, so drive carefully."

"Another case?" Bob asked. "Not another lost kid?"

"No, nothing like that," Wade told him. "Just some routine stuff we need to check out before we head down the mountain."

Bob gathered his family up and herded them towards his truck and camper. "Come on, boys, let's get out of here. We can talk on the way home." He shook hands with everyone and climbed into the cab of his truck. "Thanks for everything," he called as he backed around onto the road. "Good luck."

Andee turned to Wade and Brian. "Are you up to more, or do you want to head to town for traffic control and evacuation?"

Wade looked at Brian and shrugged. "Might as well go the whole distance," he said and winked. "I think they've pretty much got things handled down there."

Andee nodded ascent and introduced Morgan to the deputies as they climbed back into her

Tahoe. "Buckle up, boys. Ren says it's a rough road up the mountain."

On the way up the narrow log road, Andee filled the two in on what the firefighters had found. Not knowing exactly how much Morgan wanted to share of his cases, she let him tell the deputies why he was with her and what he suspected. She was glad to hear he held very little back from her deputies. It showed trust in her integrity for the men she hired in her office.

They arrived on the scene fifteen minutes later. The glow of the encroaching forest fire looked closer as darkness deepened. Ren had taped out the scene. He met them when they arrived. Five minutes later, Carlie Matthews drove up in her Jeep.

Carlie was the county's evidence technician. She was a fairly new addition to the Sheriff's Office. Most of the time she spent in the office, organizing and recording evidence for court cases, but she was qualified to investigate crime scenes and collect evidence as well. Ren guided her under the yellow tape at a point where evidence would not be destroyed and up the incline to the brush pile.

Ren explained how the firefighters had come upon the scene. "I've photographed everything around the scene," he told her. "I took statements from the firefighters. They're going to be tied up for a while with this monster."

Carlie stooped under the pile of brush. Part of the black bag had been torn away by animals. She unzipped and shone her light into the face of a blond woman.

"Did you collect any evidence from around the body?" she asked Ren.

"I didn't find anything but some tracks," he told her, "and they were filled in with sand from the wind. Tire tracks were the same. Only one other set, and that was the engine the fire crew was driving. Not much help."

"Okay," Carlie bit her lip and shone her light around the tape. "Let's get these deputies and the sheriff up here to canvas the area in case you missed anything. If that fire keeps moving this way, there won't be a crime scene left by morning. Let's find what we can, then get out of here. Did you notify the mortuary?"

A vehicle pulled up behind the sheriff's unit as she finished speaking. "Yes, ma'am. I think that may be him there."

Carlie called to the sheriff and she, Morgan and her deputies moved up the slope. "We need to cover the area and collect what evidence we can, if there is any, and get out of here. The fire is inching closer every minute, and I do not want to be caught up here in the middle of it. Sheriff, can you get the mortuary guy to get the body out of here? Ren took pictures while there was still light, so we'll have that. Maybe, just maybe, there will be something left behind."

Everyone moved into position. Two men from the mortuary moved up the slope with a stretcher. Carlie recognized them as men she had worked with before, so she didn't waste her breath telling them procedure.

Strong flashlight beams crisscrossed each other as they searched the area for any bit of evidence that might give a clue as to who the woman was and who had dumped her body. After the body had been carried down the hill, Carlie and Andee stooped down under the brush and searched the area intently. They were backing out, when Andee's light caught a slight gleam coming from the far side of where the body had lain. She held up a hand and cautiously moved back under the limbs. Gently brushing the dirt away she used her finger to move a bit of dirt away from the object in question. A small, round, brown tube-like object lay exposed in the sand. Andee scooped her fingers under it and dumped it, dirt and all, into the small bag Carlie pulled from a pouch on her hip. Carlie smiled.

"Looks like a handle that screws onto something." She shrugged. "But at least it's something,"

Andee grinned.

"Yes," Carlie said. "Now, let's get out of here!"

Her gaze turned to the horizon. What had been an orange-red glow only moments before was now flames, rising up above the ridge. Suddenly a huge ball of flame shot into the sky and landed 500 yards from their position. The dry pine needles and grass immediately ignited a spot fire and began licking the fuel around it.

"That's too close. Let's get out of here. We'll have to work with what we have." Andee pushed down the hill, calling to the men to follow.

Chapter 13

Thursday night

Get Out Now!

A pounding and voices from below the hatch door on the tower room caused Amy Holland to sit upright on her cot. It took her only a moment to orient herself. She was in her tower. But why was it so light? She'd turned out the lights when she went to bed. Her startled mind raced as she remembered why she'd stayed at the tower. Flames licked at the trees less than a half mile away on two sides.

The pounding began again. "Amy! Are you in there? Amy! Wake up! Amy!" She recognized the voices of John Wilson and Steve Connors.

She hurried to the hatch and pushed the heavy chest off the door. After unhooking the latches, she moved back and allowed the men below to shove the door open. She began throwing her meager belongings into her back pack, even as the men shouted that she had to leave.

After securing her own personal belongings she looked around the tower to see if there was anything she could save in the small room.

"We don't have time, Amy," John yelled. "Go, go, go." He pushed her towards the hatch and practically shoved her down the steps.

"You have your truck?" And then before she could respond, he led her to it. Holding his hands out for her keys, he unlocked it and helped her inside. "You're going to brush real close to the fire on your way out of here! You know how the road goes. You'll be driving towards the fire. Keep going, no matter what! We'll be right behind you. When you hit the 249, turn left! I want you to drive down the 261, you hear? It's faster and safer!"

Amy nodded and bit her lip.

"Remember, don't stop for anything! We're right behind you! Now go!"

Amy turned the key in the ignition. The starter made a grinding sound. "No, no, not now!" she groaned. "Come on." She turned the key again. More grinding. She needed a new starter but had hoped it would hold up until payday.

"Oh, Dear Lord," she prayed. "Please let it start. Please, please."

John Wilson bailed out of the cab of his engine truck.

"Amy? Don't tell me. You still haven't replaced that starter?" His face held more concern than anger, for which Amy was glad, but she knew he thought her foolish for putting it off yet again.

She turned the key once more. There was a grinding, then the smooth whir as the starter caught and the engine started. She breathed a quick thank you to God in the heavens, offered up a silent prayer that the truck would not die on the way out of there, smiled a broad, yet nervous smile at John, gave him a thumbs-up and shoved the truck in gear. Backing out, she headed down the rocky, rutted road towards the blazing inferno that threatened everything in its path.

She rounded the first curve, and gasped as a wall of flame greeted her. Tongues of flame licked at the edge of the road. Even as she watched, the fire traveled above her across the road into the treetops overhead. She was surrounded by fire. Behind her the headlights of the engine truck gleamed, urging her on, pushing her. The road straightened and she accelerated. She screamed when a small, burning limb fell across the hood of her truck and spiraled off onto the side of the road, scattering embers and immediately starting a blaze in the dead, dry grasses alongside.

Gripping the wheel tightly she made the next turn, skidding sideways over the rocks.

"Oh dear Lord," she prayed silently as she careened around another curve."Please get us out of here." Another, larger limb fell on the road in front of her. She wrenched the wheel and felt the tumultuous grind as the truck rose on two wheels. For a moment she thought she had lost it and would end up rolling down the steep mountainside, but the truck righted. The wheels gained purchase and she sighed. She was almost to the junction now. Fire was ahead of her, behind her and to her left. Thankfully, the way out was to the right.

She made a right at the first junction, then a left a half a mile later. Only a couple of miles to go to the 261. John and his crew stayed close behind her. The smoke swirled, blurring her vision. Her nostrils and eyes stung and she could feel the heat all around her. Just before she reached the 261 junction, John blinked his lights at her and she pulled to the side of the road. He pulled up alongside and Steve Connors rolled his window down.

John yelled to her from across the cab of the truck. "Good girl! Now, get down that road and don't stop! When you get to town, go home and stay there. I've let dispatch know you're on your way down. Call her when you get there. I'll see you in a day or two."

"You aren't going down?"

"No. Got a couple of things we gotta do up here. Now, go!" His voice became softer, but she could still hear him across the sound of both truck engines. "And Amy, be careful, okay?"

She smiled weakly, gave him a thumbs up and accelerated down the highway, thankful that this portion was blacktop all the way to Round Valley.

She had left the fire behind her, but the urgency she felt while careening around curves with the fire hot above and behind did not dissipate until she was halfway down the mountain. She felt somewhat forlorn not having the lights of Engine 62 behind her.

When she reached the 260 highway a sheriff's deputy was blocking the southbound lane. She pulled in beside his unit and recognized Jared McCormick. She'd gone to school with him and had even dated him a couple of times.

"Amy," Jared acknowledged her. "Where'd you come from? We've had this road blocked all day."

She gave him a shaky smile. "I know. I went up yesterday morning. I work the Big Lake Lookout."

"You were still there tonight?"

"Up until about an hour ago. John Wilson's crew rousted me out of my bed and got me out of the tower just in time."

"Has it reached Big Lake yet?"

"No, not yet. It's on the back side and to the east. The tower is probably gone by now. If it's not, it will be by morning."

"If not, it will be by morning."

Amy heard the tremor in her voice and before she could stop them, tears filled her eyes. Big Lake Lookout Tower had been her summer home for seven years. She'd spent nights there. Brought friends up to see the view. Showed numerous children and adults how to use the fire finder, explained to them, her job as a fire lookout. She'd made contact with people from all walks of life; teachers, scout leaders, hikers, locals and flatlanders. There had been nice people and belligerent ones. Some returned summer after summer and she welcomed them. Others had given her the willies. She'd made friends. Lasting friends. Friends who called her from various parts of the state at different times to inquire about her life and even pray with her.

She knew in her heart of hearts that this last day and night would be the last she would ever spend there as a fire lookout.

"I need to get home, Jared," she gulped. "You be safe, okay?"

She put her truck in gear and eased out on SR260 highway.

She arrived at her small trailer just five minutes

later. She was exhausted, but she knew she would not be able to sleep. She filled a kettle with water and turned on the burner. While the water heated, she ran a warm bath and gathered up fresh pajamas. Returning to the kitchen, she made herself a cup of chamomile tea, and made her way back to the bathroom. The tears she had held back since talking to Jared began as she undressed and stepped into the tub. They continued for a long time.

Finally, an hour later, teacup dry and bathwater past being warm, she forced herself to get out and dry off. Donning pajamas, she turned out the lights and made her way down the hallway to her bedroom.

She could not even pray.

Chapter 14
Monday, June 6, 2011
I Want
My Wife's Body, Now!

The residents of Alpine, thirty miles south of Round Valley awoke on Thursday morning with the fire at their back doors. Pre-evacuation orders were issued and the residents hustled to gather together the things they deemed important. By 3:00 PM the town had been evacuated. Law enforcement, firefighters and a few stubborn residents were all that was left in the villages. Nutrioso was under pre-evacuation orders and were evacuated the next day.

Now the forest service and law enforcement were speculating if Round Valley and the town of Greer, seventeen miles to the west also would have to be evacuated.

Andee's office was stretched thin. Everyone was

on duty manning road blocks, directing traffic, helping with the evacuations and answering calls. The body the firefighters had found in the mountains had been tentatively identified as Roma Montgomery, one of the missing women on Morgan Freeman's list. They were waiting on her husband for a positive I.D.

Apache County did not have a morgue, so her remains were at the only mortuary in town, awaiting a positive I.D. and for the E.T. to do a thorough investigation. However, Carlie's elderly parents lived in Alpine and Carlie had taken time off to help them evacuate and get them settled into the Red Cross shelter that had been established in Pinetop-Lakeside, fifty miles to the west.

Andee entered the back door of the sheriff's office with trepidation. It could only get worse before it got better. Stopping off at the break room, she poured herself a cup of coffee, and then continued out into the main part of the building.

A man rose to meet her as she proceeded towards her office door. Andee raised a questioning eyebrow towards Sandra, who immediately introduced the man advancing into the room.

"Sheriff, this is Roger Montgomery."

Andee dropped her case on Sandra's desk and stretched out her hand towards the man. He grasped it in a wimpy half shake. Andee wiped her hand on her trousers before she could stop herself.

"Mr. Montgomery. I'm sorry for your loss, sir."

The man hardly acknowledged her condolences. "You're sure it's my wife? Where did you find her?"

Andee avoided answering him directly. "We appreciate you coming all this way. I know it's a long drive. Can I get you some refreshment?"

"No. I just need to make sure it's my wife and make arrangements for her funeral. Where's the mortuary?"

Andee picked up her case and headed to her office. "I'll need to call the mortician to make sure he's free," she told him. "Then I'll take you there." She brushed past him and unlocked her office door. She closed it firmly behind her, and set her case on the corner of her desk. As she reached for the phone, she saw the red light on her private line blinking and pressed it.

"Good morning, this is the sheriff."

"Andee."

"Daddy, hi. Is anything wrong?"

Her father sighed. "I just wanted you to know your mom and I are going up to Flagstaff for a few days. This smoke is really bothering your mother and I want to get her out of it."

"It's really been thick, hasn't it? I'm glad you're going. I suspect they'll be calling for evacuations today or tomorrow You know Alpine and Nutrioso have already been evacuated?"

"We've been monitoring the radio. I didn't want to bother you. I know you're busy," her father said.

"Oh, Daddy, I'm sorry…"

"No, no. Honey, I know how busy you've been. I just wanted you to know, so you wouldn't worry about us. We're going to stay with Max and Jean. I'll call you when we get there."

"Drive safely, okay?"

"I will. Bye, honey."

"Bye, Daddy."

Andee hung up and made the call to the mortuary.

———— ◈ ————

Bruce Botswell, the owner of the local mortuary greeted the pair at the door. After introductions, he indicated a room off to the side of the main room with a large table and chairs in its center.

"If you'll wait right here, I'll get your wife ready for you to see her," the mortician said. He left through a back door.

Andee indicated that Montgomery should sit. "It'll take a few minutes for him to get her ready. You can make arrangements to have her transported when our examination is over."

"Examination?"

"Your wife, if this is your wife, was murdered. My Evidence Technician will examine her body for any clues as to who could have done this to her, and then she will be sent to Tucson to the medical examiner to determine cause of death."

"So, what's the holdup? You've had her here since Friday, haven't you?"

"Since Thursday, sir. You may have noticed we have a major wildfire in the area. We barely made it out with your wife's body on Thursday night before the fire encompassed the entire area. Another hour and it's doubtful her body would ever have been found. Since Thursday night the fire has grown to almost a quarter of a million acres. My office has been extremely busy. Our E.T. will probably examine your wife's body today. As soon as her examination is done, we will send her to the Medical Examiner's office in Tucson for an autopsy to determine cause of death. After that, she can be released so you may finalize arrangements for her."

"You mean I have to wait until all that is done before I can make funeral arrangements?"

"Unfortunately a forest fire does not wait for the everyday business of mere men. My deputies are working around the clock to ensure the safety of

Round Valley citizens. They are now talking about a mandatory evacuation of the entire town. If mandatory evacuation is ordered, it may be another week before I can release your wife's body, sir. I would suggest you make arrangements with Mr. Botswell for your wife to be transported to the funeral home of your choice when we release her, and go home to your children."

Montgomery's face turned red with anger.

"What a stupid jerk water town. So it could be a week or more?"

"You do want to find out who killed your wife, don't you Mr. Montgomery?"

Andee watched as his face blanched. He swallowed hard. "Of course I do. But we already know it was whoever kidnapped those other women from those other mortuaries. Find them, and you'll find my wife's killer."

"I certainly hope you are right, sir. But your wife's body may offer some evidence that we wouldn't find otherwise in our pursuit of these guys. Just go back to the valley. Be with your children. Keep in touch with Mr. Botswell. He will keep you informed and arrange for delivery of your wife's body as soon as possible."

Andee's cell phone rang. She looked at the read out. It was Sandra. "I have to take this. Mr. Montgomery, Bruce will take care of you. Please just go back to Phoenix. We are probably going to be evacuating the entire town today or tomorrow. You'd be best at home until things settle down here."

She turned quickly and left the room.

"Sheriff," Sandra Bradley said, as soon as she answered her phone. "Morgan Freeman is on the line. Says it's important."

"Do you have a number, Sandra?" she jotted it down and told Sandra to tell Freeman she would call him right back.

She turned back into the room where Roger Montgomery waited. "Mr. Montgomery, if you'll excuse me. We'll let you know as soon as something develops."

She shoved the mortuary door open and headed for her vehicle. "Morgan," she tried to sound calm and controlled as she answered the phone. "What can I do for you?"

"I've heard from Penny," he said.

"Your niece? The one who was kidnapped? When? Where is she?"

"As far as I can tell, somewhere in the vicinity of St. Johns. There was a message on my machine when I got home this morning. The time stamp says she called Thursday, about the time we were picking up the Montgomery woman. I went into Show Low to follow up on the charges on Melba Webster's credit card. I stayed with friends and just got home this morning. Let me play the message for you. Hold on a minute."

She waited and listened as Morgan shuffled around. "Okay, here it is."

A young girl's voice trembled over the machine. *"Uncle Morgan,"* Penny spoke quickly. *"It's Penny. I'm okay. I'm with a woman named Melba Webster. They are holding us in the basement of an old house about three miles east of St. Johns. Or at least I think it is St. Johns. I'm going back to be with Melba because I don't know what they will do to her if they find I'm gone. Uncle Morgan..."* The recording stopped.

"That's it. The rest was personal. Just to tell her folks she's okay. How well do you know St. Johns?"

"Well, enough. Town proper, anyway. I have a couple of deputies over there that can probably fill us in with the area east of town proper. Did Penny say how she got away to make the call?"

"No! She just said she was going back to the other woman. Sheriff...Andee.... Could you hold off about calling your deputy over there? I mean, just until we can check it out ourselves?"

"I don't think that's a good idea. Look, I'm tied up here with fire traffic and it'll take you at least half an hour to get over here, and another half hour to get to St. Johns. When did you say she called? We're talking precious time here."

"No. Listen. Can we go out there, just the two of us? Scout around before we call out the posse?"

"What are you not telling me?" she demanded.

He sighed. Penny had said she thought the sheriff was involved. Morgan shook his head. He just couldn't see Andee involved in a kidnapping, or anything illegal, for that matter. Maybe Penny had misunderstood. Maybe it was a deputy. He'd been called sheriff many times when he wore a deputy's uniform. People just didn't know the difference. A uniform was a uniform.

Suddenly, he decided.

"It's just something Penny said."

"I thought you said the rest was just personal stuff. Did she leave more than one message?"

Andee chewed the inside of her cheek.

"Look, Morgan. It's already been four days since she left the message. Are you sure you want to leave it that long? I could have one of my guys check it out right now. What if they move them? Maybe they have already. You were a cop. You know time is of the essence."

She heard him sigh. "I know you're right. And my sister would never forgive me if anything happened to Penny now that we know she was alive on Thursday night. Okay, call your deputy, but I want to be there when you go in."

"Okay. Why don't you head on over here and I'll free up a couple of hours. But Morgan, you'd better come clean when you get here."

"I will. It's just a gut feeling I have. Can we just go with that?"

Andee stifled a smile, even though he couldn't see her through the phone. *'That gut-feeling. When you were a cop, you couldn't argue with the gut.'*

She had barely settled into her office chair when Sandra buzzed her from the front desk. "Mr. Montgomery is here."

"I'll be right out." She frowned. "I can't seem to reach Apache-12. Do you know if he's on duty?" She was referring to James "Tubby" O'Toole, a deputy serving the northern part of the county and the St. John area. Growing up he had been short and over-weight. Today, however; he was string-bean slender and almost six and a half feet tall. Despite his tall frame, the name had stuck. He had worked under the old sheriff, coming into his office as a young kid right out of high school. He was about forty. He'd been married twice and divorced twice. Both wives had charged mental and physical abuse, but nothing had come of the charges and he remained on with the sheriff's office. He had graying hair and a dark moustache, blue eyes with heavy hooded lids. She knew he had supported Hilton Parks, although he was not allowed to campaign. She'd check the files of all the deputies under her jurisdiction and had made a mental note to watch Tubby O'Toole, but so far everything seemed on the up and up.

She had only seen him a couple of times in the short time she'd been sheriff. She had not been impressed with the handsome cop at either meeting. He was good looking and knew it. He tried, rather blatantly, to flirt with her, which she had found offensive.

"I'll call the substation over there," Sandra told her.

Andee thanked her and rose to meet Roger Montgomery. She forced a smile and greeted him as she closed her office door behind her.

"Mr. Montgomery, did you get everything worked out with Mr. Botswell?"

"Not that you care," Montgomery all but shouted at her.

"Excuse me?" Andee stood up straighter and rocked forward on her toes, preparing for battle if necessary.

"This is stupid and you know it," Montgomery snarled.

"Mr. Montgomery, I think I explained this to you before. We have a wildfire threatening our town. Your wife's remains must be examined by our Evidence

Technician and then we have to have an autopsy to determine cause of death. These things take time."

She walked past him. Suddenly he gripped her arm and halted her in her steps. She shrugged, but he held her tightly.

"Mr. Montgomery, please remove your hand from my arm." From the corner of her eye, she saw Sandra reach for the phone and press a button.

"I want my wife's body released! You will be hearing from my lawyer."

Andee looked him straight in the eye. "By all means, Mr. Montgomery, please call your lawyer. I know you're upset about your wife, but if you don't unhand me right this minute, you will need your lawyer to get you out of jail." She pulled her arm from his grasp and stepped back just as George Townsend entered the room from the back.

"Trouble Sheriff?"

"It's okay, George. Mr. Montgomery is leaving town today before they call for mandatory evacuation, aren't you Mr. Montgomery? Now if you'll excuse me. I have to make a call. Maybe you'd like an escort out of town?" She shoved past him, into her office, and then locked the door behind her. She immediately turned on the monitor that connected to the various closed circuit cameras throughout the building and pressed the button for the outer office.

She watched as George spoke softly, yet firmly to Roger Montgomery and escorted him out the door. There was a look of hatred on Montgomery's face as he left the building. Andee shuddered. *'Best watch my back when he's in town,'* she thought. *'There is more to Mr. Roger Montgomery than meets the eye.'*

Chapter 15
Monday afternoon
Meet The Former Sheriff

Morgan climbed into the Tahoe beside Andee. Fastening his seat belt, he smiled at her.

"Thanks, Sheriff."

"Don't thank me yet, Mr. Freestone." She purposely got his name wrong, but from the quirk of his lips and the quick eye-wink he threw her direction, she guessed he knew she knew it.

"Tell me about your 'gut'."

Morgan ran his hand around the brim of his hat. He looked out the side window as she pulled out onto the street, and then looked back at her.

"Penny. I didn't tell you everything. She said she thought the sheriff was involved in her kidnapping."

Andee gasped. "Me? She thinks I'm involved?"

Morgan shook his head. "She just said she

thought the sheriff was involved and that I shouldn't trust the sheriff."

"Yet here you are."

"Look, I'm sorry I wasn't completely honest with you on the phone. It's not the kind of conversation I like having on the phone. If I'm going to accuse someone, I prefer to do it face to face."

"And are you accusing me, Mr. Freeman?"

"No, I'm not. That's what I'm trying to tell you. But that's why I didn't want you to call a deputy. When I worked for Sheriff Joe in Maricopa County, people called the deputies in uniform sheriff all the time. Maybe Penny heard someone talking to a deputy. Andee, I'm following my gut here, and my gut tells me you are above and beyond kidnapping. Just sayin'."

Andee blushed. To hide her embarrassment, she flipped on her flashing lights and stepped on the accelerator. "Thanks."

They arrived at the St. Johns town limits in less than thirty minutes. Andee turned the red and blues off as they entered town.

"I'm afraid I'm going to have to call a deputy in on this," she told Morgan. "I don't know the area well enough to start a search without some local advice."

At the Main Street junction, she turned left and reached for her radio microphone.

"Wait."

"Wait?"

"I've got a hunch," Morgan told her. "Penny said she was to the east of St. Johns, so she would probably have come into town on this street."

"But how do you know she wasn't turned around? If she was blindfolded she could be turned completely around."

"No," he argued. "I know Penny. If she said east, she knew it was east. She called at about 7 PM. That means the sun was in the west. She knew it was east."

"Okay. Sooo, you just want to head east and see what we can find?"

"Yeah, but I know someone here in St. Johns. An old-timer. Maybe he can help us. Get me to a phone booth or somewhere with a phone book."

Andee pulled into the Circle K. Morgan bound out of the Tahoe and headed to the phone booth attached to the corner of the building. The phone book had been torn off the heavy cord hanging from the corner of the booth.

He turned and traversed the few feet to the door of the store, holding it open for a young woman who was coming out. Five minutes later he returned to the Tahoe.

"Okay. Let's hope he's home." He opened his cell phone and dialed the number he had written down.

"Gus!" He turned and gave Andee a thumbs up. "Hey, this is Morgan. How you doing, you old coot?" Andee could hear a raspy voice on the other end. She waited while Morgan talked to the man he called Gus. After the preliminaries, Morgan got down to the purpose of his call. Turning a page on the notebook in which he had written Gus' number, he began to write as he listened. "Okay. That's great. Sure appreciate this Gus. What's that? Yeah. Yeah. I'll let you know. Thanks. Yeah, thanks again."

"Okay. At the edge of town the highway turns north towards the Interstate." Andee nodded. "Right at that turn or really close to it is a dirt road that goes towards a salt lake over in New Mexico." Andee nodded again. "Gus said about half a mile down that road we'll find a road that veers off to the right. About a mile in on that road is old homestead. The house is kind of run down, but the owners use it sometimes in the summer when they come up."

"Let's go." Andee turned the Tahoe around and they drove back in the direction from which they had come. At the edge of town, she slowed. The dirt road Gus had mentioned was the main road for a fairly new subdivision with 'ranchettes' advertised at $5,000 and up. A half mile further in, they found the road Gus had told him about. It was hardly more than a couple of tracks and in places running water had left deep ruts. It was definitely not the kind of road one would travel in anything less than a four wheel drive vehicle. Andee stopped and she and Morgan exited the vehicle.

"Looks like there's been a bit of traffic for a homestead that's only used a couple of weeks in the summer," Morgan remarked.

They had gone a short distance when Morgan pointed ahead of them. Dust kicked up and caught the wind from a vehicle coming in their direction. Andee pulled to the side of the road and waited. Five minutes later, another sheriff's department unit appeared. It slowed, and then proceeded cautiously up beside the sheriff's Tahoe.

"Tubby." Andee greeted the deputy. It felt weird calling him Tubby, but James sounded even more foreign. "I've been trying to reach you all morning."

Tubby O'Toole smiled broadly and winked and touched the brim of hid hat. "Have you now? And what would the purty sheriff need with Tubby O'Toole. Thought that fire over your way was keeping you busy. You checking on me, Sheriff?"

She felt Morgan tense, then force himself to relax.

"No. Not checking on you Tubby. Just needed you to check on a couple of things for me. But we're here now," she motioned towards Morgan, indicating she was not alone. "We'll check it out. I'll expect a full report of your activities today, Deputy."

O'Toole sucked in a breath. "A full report? Sure sheriff. I always fill out the duty log. What are you looking for in our fair town?"

"What's down this road?" she asked him.

"This road? Not much. An old homestead that belongs to the Blanton family. They seldom use it. Someone reported they'd seen some lights here a couple of nights ago. I thought I'd check it out, but I didn't find anything."

"You call the Blantons to see if any family members were staying there?"

"No ma'am. Thought I'd check it out first. Looks like a couple of cars been in there. I figure kids, probably. No broken windows or anything, though."

She smiled her brightest smile. "They'll probably be evacuating Round Valley today or tomorrow. You're going to have an influx of evacuees, although many will be going to the Red Cross shelter over in Pinetop-Lakeside. Keep in touch with the office, will you?"

"Yes ma'am." She waited until O'Toole was out of sight before pulling back onto the rutted two track road and continuing on.

"That, Mr. Freeman, was Tubby O'Toole. Apache County Deputy for almost 20 years. What do you think he was doing out here?"

"You didn't believe him?"

She smiled. "Maybe. Did you?"

Ten minutes later they approached an old dilapidated farm house. At one time it had been white, but the paint was peeling and the planks were graying due to years of exposure to the elements. Curtains sagged at the windows. From the front of the house, there was no evidence of a basement. Andee parked the Tahoe.

"What do you think?" she asked as her feet hit the ground. She and Morgan stopped and examined the tire tracks in the sand beside her Tahoe. They quickly recognized the tracks belonging to the other Tahoe. They were fresh, but it looked as if they or a similar vehicle had been there previously. Booted footprints went from the side of the vehicle up the steps. They followed the tracks around the house and back to the vehicle. It was impossible to tell if he had entered the house, or just returned to the vehicle.

Andee walked up onto the front porch. She tried the door, but it was solid.

Behind her, Morgan sauntered around the corner of the building. He'd barely disappeared around it when she heard him whistle and call her name. She rounded the corner and saw him pulling tumble weeds away from a window at ground level. The wind had blown them tightly against the side of the building so they had not seen the window while they were following the tracks of the deputy.

"Penny, are you in there?" Morgan tapped lightly on the window. "Penny, it's Uncle Morgan." And then in a whisper, Andee heard him say, "Please dear Jesus, let them be here. Oh, God, I hope I'm not too late."

Placing her flashlight against the dirty window pane, Andee knelt beside Morgan and cupped her hands around her eyes in order to see into the dark basement below. She was about to turn away, when she thought she caught a movement in the corner of the room.

"Penny Dixon, Melba Wilson, are you in there? This is Sheriff Andee Taylor. Penny, I have your Uncle with me. Penny, are you there?"

She looked at Morgan. "I think there is something or someone down there, but they aren't going to answer me."

Again she perceived a small movement in the corner of the room, but there was no answer. Morgan touched her arm. "Come on. I've got an idea." He pulled her away from the window and walked back up on the front porch. He reached above the door and ran his fingers across the door post. Coming away empty-handed, he moved to the window on the right and repeated procedure, then to the window to the left. He had reached the far edge when something fell from the ledge and landed on the porch, bouncing and finding a crack in the floorboards.

"No!" He kicked at the key, trying to stop it from reaching the crack, but it seemed to have a mind of its own. Dropping to one knee, he peered into the crack. "Not enough room to crawl under there." He looked up, but he was talking to empty air.

Andee was at the Tahoe, opening the back. She rummaged in her tool box and returned to him carrying a claw hammer. She handed it to him. "Think you can pull a nail?" she grinned.

Five minutes later, they had the elusive key in hand. "How'd you know there would be a key?" Andee asked.

Morgan shrugged. "Luck and reasoning. Different family members use the place from time to time. Leave the key in the off chance someone forgets to bring theirs. My grandma used to leave hers for me over the window sill. She said everyone looks for a key over the door post, but few look for one over the window sill."

"Well, what are we waiting for?" Andee reached for the key, but he held it firmly in his hand.

"You're the law," he told her. "I'll open, you clear." Andee nodded and unholstered her weapon. Morgan bent and raised his pant leg, removing a 38 caliber Smith and Wesson from a leg holster. Andee raised an eyebrow. "What? I've got a permit," he told her, but she just nodded and grinned. He put the key into the lock on the front door.

He pushed the door open and Andee entered, swinging her weapon from side to side. Morgan followed her in. Two doors led off of the main room. Andee motioned for Morgan to take the door on the right and she headed for the door on the left, which led to the kitchen area. The kitchen was a large farm-style kitchen. Countertop and cabinets lined one wall with a single porcelain sink situated under the window. At the end of the counter, near the door was a gas range and on the opposite wall was a wood cooking stove, complete with warming oven and water reservoir. A small wooden table sat between the wood stove and an old 60's model refrigerator. The kitchen table filled the center of the room. A doorway to what looked like a short hallway led off the kitchen to her right. She was about to enter the hallway, when Morgan appeared at the end.

"All clear," he whispered.

Two doors, directly across from each other, opened off the hallway. The one to the right was the bathroom. Silently they nodded to each other. Morgan tried the door on the left. It was locked. He frowned, but ran his hand above the door frame and extracted a skeleton key. Fitting it into the lock, he pushed the door open.

A set of steep stairs led downward into a cellar. He flipped the switch on the wall beside the door, but nothing happened. He shrugged and mouthed, "It was worth a try."

Andee turned on her flashlight, and with weapon still drawn, she crept down the stairs, staying close to the wall. Morgan followed close behind. At the bottom of the stairs, Andee turned the beam of her flashlight around the small 10' x 10' room. Unlike many cellars in these old farm houses, this one was finished with concrete walls and floor. The dirty window at ceiling level barely let in enough light to see, but as her eyes became adjusted, she was able to see a bed against one wall, a small table and two chairs. Heaped in the corner, against the wall where she thought she'd seen movement before was a pile of blankets. Moving closer she gingerly pulled at the corner, lifting and then jerking it from the pile.

She gasped. "Morgan!" But he was right behind her.

"Penny! Oh, sweetie, are you okay?" Lying on top of and buried under the pile of blankets were the two women they had been seeking. Both were bound and gagged. Both struggled to get up, but they were bound together and could not move. Morgan holstered his weapon in the special leg holster and dug his hand in his pocket, extracting a pocket knife. Opening the blade, he dropped to one knee and cut the cords binding the two women together. Andee dropped down beside him and carefully removed the duct tape that sealed their mouths.

When Penny was free she flung her arms around Morgan's neck, sobbing and laughing. "I didn't think you would find us in time," she cried. "It's been days since I left you that message. I thought we would die here. Oh, Uncle Morgan, I was so scared."

Morgan shushed her and patted her back in comfort. Lifting her gingerly off the floor, he held her to steady her shaking legs. "It's okay, darlin'. You're okay now. It's alright. Can you stand?"

In answer she crumpled, but he caught her up and placed her gently on the edge of the bed. "Take it easy. Give it time."

Meanwhile, Andee was ministering to Melba Wilson who cried silently. Tears poured down her face and she beamed a smile of gratitude at Andee, but no sounds came from her lips or throat. Andee rubbed her legs and arms to help the circulation, smiling reassuringly at the woman as she worked.

After what seemed like a long time, but had probably been only ten minutes, Andee's eyes met Morgan's as he continued to hold and console his niece. "Can you help me get her up?" she asked him.

Making sure Penny could sit upright without falling, Morgan knelt beside Andee. "Well, Melba, we've been pretty concerned about you. Do you think you can stand if I help you?"

Melba nodded and offered her hands. Morgan grasped both and braced himself as he started to pull her upward. A sudden gasp of pain escaped her lips and he released her before she'd moved off the floor. "I think my wrist is broken," she told him.

Moving behind her and motioning for Andee to steady her, he placed his hands under her arm pits and gently raised her to her feet. Slowly they walked to the bed and he helped her to sit on the edge of it beside his niece.

"Uncle Morgan," Penny whispered. "Do you think we could just get out of this cellar? They might come back. Please?"

Morgan caught Andee's eye and she nodded. "Sure, Sweetie. Why don't you go on up with the sheriff and I'll follow once Mrs. Wilson is able to walk."

Penny looked doubtfully from Morgan to Andee. "It's okay," Morgan told her. "The sheriff is a good guy. Seriously." Still not looking completely convinced, she cautiously moved towards the stairs.

"You're right behind us, right?"

"I'll be there soon. Just go with the sheriff. She'll

take good care of you."

As soon as they reached the top of the stairs, Morgan turned his attention to Melba Wilson. There was a half empty bottle of water on the small table by the bed. Unscrewing the cap, he held the bottle to her lips. Her left hand came up to support the bottle. When she had taken a few swallows, she pushed the bottle away. "Save some for Penny," she rasped. "She's not had any water in days."

Morgan smiled at her. "You don't worry about Penny. The sheriff will take good care of her."

"Are you sure?" Her voice quivered. "We heard some of those men talking to the Sheriff. It sounded like the sheriff was the one in charge. But we thought the sheriff was a man."

"Did you actually hear the sheriff talk?"

"I'm not sure. We just heard men talking and once in a while they would call someone 'sheriff.' We didn't hear a woman's voice, though."

"You just rest," Morgan reassured her. "We'll discuss everything as soon as we get you taken care of. Do you think you can walk now?"

Melba stood cautiously to her feet. Morgan grasped her left elbow to steady her. Moving around behind her, he took hold of her right arm at the elbow. "I'm going to leave your left hand free so you can balance and help yourself up the stairs, and I'm going to steady the right one. Hopefully, we won't jar it too much. Okay? Ready?"

Melba nodded and took her first wobbly step. When they reached the bottom of the stairs, she stood looking upwards. Grasping the rail against the wall with her left hand and smiling weakly at Morgan, she placed her foot on the first step.

Suddenly the door above them slammed shut. They heard Penny scream and Andee's startled exclamation. Morgan pulled Melba back against him, and swung her away from the stairs, gently placing her behind him and steadying her against the wall.

"Wait, here," he whispered. Silently he crept up the stairs and cautiously tried the door. The knob turned, but the door had been locked. Moving back down the stairs, he helped Melba to the bed and instructed her to rest. Removing the 38 from his ankle holster, he shoved it in the waistband of his pants.

Overhead he could faintly hear the mumble of raised voices and the clomp of feet across the wooden floor boards.

"Didn't Penny say she got out of here through this window the night she called me?"

Melba nodded. "I wish she hadn't come back. I told her not to."

Morgan smiled a lopsided smile at her. "I've known Penny all her life, and she is pretty headstrong.

I doubt there is anything you could have said that would have made her leave you alone here. Don't you worry about it. We'll get you out of here."

He unlatched the window and pulled a chair over to it. Something fell, crashing to the floor over head. He wished he knew what was going on up there. He was pretty sure the men who had kidnapped these two women had returned to the house and caught Andee unaware, while she was caring for Penny. He heard again a scream that sounded like Penny and faint cursing from a man.

Stepping up on to the chair, he peered out the dirty window before opening it. Nothing stirred, and he knew the kitchen window was on the other side of the house. It would be a tight squeeze, but if he could get out, he might be able to get back into the house and get the drop on whoever was there.

Melba was standing beside him as he lifted the window. She handed him a small, stick, about 18-inches long. It had a fork in the end which he placed on the window sill and braced the other end against the window pane to hold it up.

"It looks smoky out there," Melba said.

Morgan nodded. "Yes ma'am. There's a huge wildfire to the south of Round Valley. They will probably be evacuating the town today or tomorrow."

"Oh, my," Melba breathed. "Be careful, please."

Chapter 16
Monday afternoon
Waiting On Penny

Pushing his head and shoulders out the window, Morgan looked both ways before hoisting himself up through the narrow opening. He felt Melba's hand, pushing on his boot as he wiggled and squirmed out on his belly. Clearing the window, he pushed himself up against the wall and leaned down.

"Close the window and stay out of sight," he told Melba. "I'll be back to get you as soon as I can. Rest. Don't worry." He waited until the window closed behind him. Pulling the 38 from his waistband, he held it ready to use. Standing against the side of the building, his eyes searched the area surrounding the house. A dilapidated shed and corral fence about 200 yards away seemed his best bet for cover, but getting there would put him in plain view of the bedroom window, and if anyone was on the back porch, they might see him from the corner of the house. He moved cautiously to the front of the house. Andee's Tahoe stood where she had parked it. Behind it, blocking it on one side and behind were two other vehicles. He could only see one of them plainly. A black Dodge with tinted windows. The other could possibly be a Jeep, but the Tahoe hid it from view, so he couldn't be sure.

Easing around the corner of the house, he spied one man, leaning against the porch railing, his back to Morgan. A voice called from inside the house and the man turned and hurried inside.

Morgan debated on whether to follow the man inside and rely on the element of surprise, or wait until he knew for sure what he was facing. He heard scuffling and footsteps and jumped back around the corner of the building, just as the man came through the door, pushing Penny ahead of him. She was squirming and fighting all the way. They had not restrained her and she was not going peaceably. She sagged against her captor. He grasped her arms and raised her up, pushing her ahead of him. She stumbled, and fell face forward as she stepped off the porch. Morgan thought it looked like she had done it on purpose and was even surer of it, when the man holding her, tried to regain his balance and fell over her onto the dirt below. Penny was up and running in the opposite direction, before the man could regain his feet. He yelled and another man hit the door, shoving Andee ahead of him.

He cursed. "Go after her, you dimwit! Don't let her get away!"

He shoved Andee down the steps ahead of him, but stayed back a few steps. "And don't try anything funny like your little friend just did."

Andee moved off the porch towards the vehicles. "Stop right there," the man told her. Stopping on the edge of the porch, he watched the other man chasing Penny through the trees and shrubs. Penny was at a disadvantage, having been immobile and tied up for so long, but she had youth and determination on her side.

Morgan stepped away from the side of the house, hoping Andee would see him in her peripheral vision. She did. "How many?" he mouthed to her. She lifted three fingers against her belt. She eased back one step and then another, towards the vehicles. Before she had gone five steps, the man whirled on her, brought up his gun and fired. Morgan saw her flinch and fall. Stepping around the corner, he aimed and squeezed the trigger. The big man uttered an "oof" sound and fell to the porch. Morgan was poised for another shot, moving quickly towards Andee, when something hit him from behind, knocking him down. He rolled and came up, but he'd lost his grip on his weapon.

Turning, he saw the third man. The man on the porch was not getting up, but Andee was moving slightly. The third man aimed a gun at Morgan, circling around on the porch; he knelt beside the fallen man.

Morgan chanced moving cautiously towards Andee and knelt beside her, keeping a watch on the man with the gun. Andee held her chest with both hands, sucking breath after labored breath into her lungs. There was no blood oozing from between her fingers. Morgan helped her to sit. "Are you hit?" he asked.

Andee winced. "Vest," she said. "Hurts like a sonofagun."

The man on the porch was talking in low tones to the man Morgan had shot.

"Hey, you," he yelled at Morgan. "Leave her alone and get over here."

At first Morgan hesitated, but Andee gave him a shove. "You should go. I'm good."

Reaching the porch, the man with the gun stood back. "Get him up," he demanded.

Morgan moved up behind the man lying in a pool of blood. His bullet had entered the right side, under the ribs. It looked like a through and through, and it was bleeding profusely. Placing his arms under the man's armpits he managed to pull him into an upright position. The man was an older man, not too tall. Morgan judged that he weighed about 290 pounds. Without help, getting him to a standing position was not going to be easy. That is, even if the man could stand, once he got him up.

While debating with himself about the best way to manage the feat, he heard Penny scream. Looking over his shoulder, he saw her kicking and scratching at the man who had overtaken her and was hauling her back. He almost grinned, despite the seriousness of the situation. She was giving the man a run for his money.

Reaching the clearing, Penny saw Andee still sitting on the ground and Morgan kneeling beside the man on the porch. With renewed abandon, she lashed out with her foot and caught the tall man holding her just above the boot. He loosed his hold on her slightly and she swung with the other foot, catching him between the legs. It was his turn to scream. Falling to his knees, Penny doubled a fist and hit him across the ear, shoving him down as she pummeled his face and kicked him fiercely.

Morgan waited, watching for an opening, but before he could move, the man holding the gun pulled up and fired in the direction of his niece, then turned the barrel of the pistol back at Morgan. The man grinned. "Don't even think about it." And then to the girl who stood frozen above the man she had attacked. "You get over here honey or next one might even hit you. Might even kill you. Come on." He waved the pistol in her direction, motioning for her to stand by Andee.

"Okay, now you, Mr. Hotshot, get the boss up and get him in the house. And let's not have any more diversions, okay? Tiller," he yelled at the other man. "Get over here and help."

The man called Tiller gingerly got to his feet. Holding himself, and stumbling, he moved toward them. He climbed the porch slowly and moved up beside Morgan. Morgan grinned at the man and laughed. "Kinda met your match, didn't you?"

"Shut your face!" the man called Tiller shouted at him. The man holding the gun grunted.

"Shut up, both of you." To Tiller he said, "The boss is bleeding. Help get him into the house."

"I'll take the front, you take the back," Morgan told Tiller as he hoisted the big man's shoulders and waited for Tiller to get his feet. Inside he was still marveling at the tenacity of his niece. That was one fighting little girl.

They managed to get the 'boss' back into the house and on the bed in the bedroom. Behind them, the man with the gun herded Andee and Penny into the room.

"You know first aid, Sheriff?"

Andee nodded. "Some. But he's bleeding a lot. You need to get him to the hospital."

"Yeah, right. That's just what he needs. A hospital. You'd like that, wouldn't you? Only if he goes to the hospital, you won't be going with him. You won't be going nowhere."

"What's that supposed to mean?"

"Look, sister, I didn't plan any of this, okay? The boss there, he was going to just leave those two women here to starve to death and he and that worthless son of his was going to Canada or somewhere. Then he stopped at Circle K in town and talked to that Tubby O'Toole and decided he'd best come out here and ensure his little nest hadn't been found."

Andee had moved to the bed and was pulling the big man's shirt out of his pants.

"That's all a bit irrelevant right now. If we're going to keep him from bleeding to death, I need some towels and some water."

"Tiller, check the bathroom. Get some towels or whatever to stop the bleeding. Hurry up."

Tiller left the room and they could hear him rummaging in the closet next door. He came out with towels and dumped them on the bed.

"I'll get water from the truck," he said and left

the room.

Andee grabbed a towel. Rolling it up, she placed it under the man on the bed at the exit site of the bullet wound. Rolling another, she placed pressure on the entry site. Penny had moved to Morgan's side. He stood beside her, but as much as he wanted to put his arm around her and comfort her, he restrained himself. There was no sense in giving them any more leverage.

"Morgan, Penny," Andee said. "I'd like you to meet the illustrious former sheriff of Apache County, Hilton Parks." She indicated the man on the bed. "And you," she gazed at the man doing the talking and holding the gun. "I believe you are Amos Murphy, former Navajo County deputy. And Tiller there," she nodded in the direction of the front door, "that would be Austin Tiller. Weren't the two of you arrested in that Connie Parks bust a year or so back?"

"I didn't have nuthin' to do with that meth thing," Murphy said. "That was all Parks and Tiller."

"Sure it was," Andee breathed. "And I'm sure you had nothing to do with kidnapping three women, stealing records or murdering one of them."

"Hey, we didn't… there were only two women, not three, and we didn't…the sheriff didn't have nuthin' to do with that murder, neither. That's why he was leaving the country. The sheriff heard about you finding that other woman murdered up in the woods. He said he wasn't going down for that."

"Shut up, you knuckle head," Parks snarled from the bed. "Where's Tiller?"

"Out to the truck to get some water so we can fix you up, boss."

"Get these two to the cellar. And secure it good, this time. Where's the other woman? The old lady?"

"I don't know, boss," Murphy told him. "I haven't seen her. This young one is the only one that got out of the cellar."

Penny stepped forward. "Where's the old woman," she raised her voice. "The old woman? She's dead, That's what! You murdering, conniving, stupid, idiot men killed her! You don't want to face murder charges? Well you're too late for that! How long did you think she would last without water or food? A week? Two? She died last night! And it's all your fault! I hope you all go to jail for a very long time. No! I hope you get the death penalty for what you did to us, and to Mrs. Wilson. You're just slime!" She stomped her foot and stepped back beside Morgan. Nervous tears filled her eyes and she dashed them away.

Morgan did a double take. Melba Wilson was very much alive, though injured, when he left her. Did Penny think she would save Melba from more injury if they thought she was dead? He'd play along.

"I'm afraid Penny is right," he told the two men. "She was tied to that woman all night long."

Penny shuddered, and turned into his shoulder. "It was just so awful."

"Get these whiners out of here," the former sheriff grumbled. "Lock them back in the cellar and secure that window."

Murphy herded them all into the hallway and removed the skeleton key from above the door post. Unlocking it, he ushered them all down the stairs. Melba was nowhere in sight. Glancing into the corner where the women had been left to die, he grunted, satisfied that Melba Wilson was under the blankets where they had left her. He had barely locked the door at the top of the stairs before Morgan had unlatched the window.

"Penny, get over here, quickly." Giving her a shove through the open window, he told her. "Get to that shed out back. Hug the wall of the house until you get on the back side. Stay there until they are gone. I doubt they'll check to make sure we are all here before they leave. Now hurry, hurry! Go!" He closed the window and latched it again.

Andee was helping Melba from under the blankets where she had had the forethought to hide.

"What in the world is going on?" she asked. "I thought I heard gunshots."

Morgan watched Penny until she disappeared from sight. He turned back as Andee began explaining to Melba what had gone on above.

"I guess we were down here, so I didn't hear them when they pulled up outside," Andee said. She went on to explain that when she and Penny had reached the top of the stairs, Penny was wobbly so she had pushed her into the kitchen to a chair. Penny had barely set down, when Hilton Parks had slammed the cellar door and locked it. He'd shoved Andee off balance and taken her weapon before she could react. They had decided to move the two captives, but since only one woman was out of the cellar and the other one, they figured, too old and out of shape to escape, they planned to leave her there.

While Andee talked she retrieved a towel from the washstand in the corner of the room. After asking Morgan for his pocket knife, she cut the towel into wide strips. Enlisting Morgan's help to hold the wrist steady, she began wrapping the strips of towel around Melba's wrist. Melba winced once, but uttered nothing more as they bandaged and secured the wrist. They had barely finished when they perceived movement at the small window that provided the only light into the room. A piece of board covered the window and they heard the pounding of hammer on nail as one of the men nailed the board across the opening, blocking their only means of escape. Darkness fell upon the small basement room.

"There are candles," Melba said, "on the table there by the bed."

Andee's flashlight was still intact in her holster. She drew it out and shown the light across the room. A candle and a small box of matches lay side by side on the table. Striking a match and lighting the small candle, she switched off the flashlight and waited for their eyes to adjust to the dim light.

"Will Penny be alright out there?" Melba asked them, a look of concern on her face.

"If they didn't see her run to the shed, she should be fine," Morgan told them. "I think if they caught her, we'd know it by now."

Andee laughed. "She's definitely a spunky one." Her eyes sought Morgan's. "You must be proud of her."

Morgan smiled. "We need a plan. Sheriff, that's your category. I'm going up the stairs to see if I can hear anything." With that, he mounted the stairs, stepping gingerly up each one to minimize any creaks. Pressing his ear against the door he could hear the men quite clearly. He listened for about fifteen minutes before making his way back down the stairs to join the women.

"No indication that they know Penny is not

here," he said. "They called in another man to help move Parks. Parks says he has a doctor in his pocket and they're taking him there."

Andee watched him as he talked. He wasn't telling them everything. Moving away from the bed and Melba Wilson, she pulled him with her.

"Spill it. What else?"

"That's it."

"You're lying. What else did they say?"

"Andee," Morgan glanced at Melba before continuing. He made his way to the table and snuffed the candle. "They're going to burn the place down."

Andee stifled a gasp. "You're serious? Any suggestions, Mr. P.I.?"

"Hey, you're the sheriff." Morgan tried to keep it light if not for her sake, then at least for Melba's. "That's your department."

"Gee, thanks," she answered him.

She moved back toward Melba thinking the woman had a right to know what they were facing.

"We have a major problem, Melba. I think three heads are better than one, so I'm going to tell you what is going on and maybe we can brainstorm and get ourselves out of this mess."

As she and Morgan talked, they watched Melba. They had expected some nerves, some tears, but the woman wore a face that a poker player would be proud to possess.

"Well, there's nothing to do, but wait for Penny to get us out of this mess," Melba said with conviction.

"Penny?" Both Morgan and Andee gaped at her.

"If you didn't think she could help, then why did you shove her out of the window?" she demanded.

Morgan chuckled. "Why indeed. You're right, Melba. We just have to wait for Penny to do something."

Chapter 17
Monday afternoon
Penny's Time To Shine

Penny hugged the wall of the old house, just as her uncle had told her. She figured the men would be in the front part of the house, or at least on the kitchen side for a few moments. When she reached the west corner at the back, she peeped around the side. No movement. If she ran toward the shed at the same angle as the corner of the house, she should be able to reach it without being seen, provided they all stayed inside the house.

She set off at a run, reaching the run down shed without hearing a shout or a shot. Darting inside, she breathed a sigh of relief. Sinking to the ground, she positioned herself against a crack so she could watch the house without being seen. She had no more settled in when the screen door on the back of the house slammed and she saw a man headed her way.

O crap! They'd seen her. Crawling to the back of the shed, she pressed herself against the back wall and looked frantically for a weapon. Suddenly the board she leaned against moved. Startled, she pushed gently and wedged herself though it. She positioned it back into place, just as the man entered the shed. Stepping back, she watched as he looked around. Was he looking for her? Putting both hands on a board leaning up against the wall of the shed, he pulled it from the wall loosening the rusted nails holding it and turned back toward the house. Picking up a hammer and a small container on the porch, he rounded the house and stopped at the cellar window from which she had escaped. He began to pound nails into the board, blocking off the window as a means of escape for the rest of the prisoners.

Penny waited until she was sure he had gone back inside the house for good. Moving back into the shed, she began to plan. That old man had been wounded pretty badly. She knew he couldn't go to a hospital without explaining how he gotten shot, so maybe they would stay here until he could travel. However, those two bozos in there didn't seem capable of nursing a man back to health unless said man told them every move to make.

She needed a plan. She could not just wait around

for something to happen. Melba, Uncle Morgan and the real sheriff were depending on her. She also knew she could not get caught so that meant she had to think this through, thoroughly.

Moving again to the back of the shed, she slipped through the wall as she had done before. In the front, the radio in the sheriff's Tahoe crackled. She could not understand what was being said, but she knew they would be doing a welfare check on the sheriff if she did not report in soon. Maybe if she could get to the Tahoe, she could radio the dispatcher.

As if to squelch the thought before she'd even thought it through, she heard an engine and saw the dust of an approaching vehicle. Someone was coming. She could hope it was help, but knew better than to expect it. It was probably another of the former sheriff's cohorts.

Staying out of sight using the security of the shed to shield her, Penny began walking. She would have to circle around to the front using the cover of the trees and bushes. If she could see what was going on, maybe she could come up with a workable plan. Bending down, she picked up a sturdy stick with a small fork on one end. Her legs were still wobbly. After being tied up for two days with no food or water, it was no wonder. She leaned on the stick as she wove between the bushes and trees, staying out of sight of the house as much as possible.

She had walked for about ten minutes, circling around the small farm house when she heard another vehicle approaching. However, this one stopped, left the road and proceeded at an angle towards where she waited, watching the house. Not knowing who it was, and not trusting anyone, she made herself small and hunched down against a tree. A small bush growing beside it afforded a bit more shelter.

Whoever was driving shut off the engine. Penny dared not move. She trembled and listened intently. She heard footsteps approaching, but before she could determine from which direction they came, she was looking up at the long legs of a sheriff's deputy.

Penny gasped and slunk back against the bush where she was hiding.

"Well, looky here," the man said. He knelt down beside her. "Who are you, and what are you doing out here at the Blanton Farm? You one of those kids that's been messing around out here?"

Penny shook her head.

"Then who are you, and what are you doing out here?"

"My name's Penny," he told him. "Who are you? What are you doing out here?"

"Well, little missy. I'm a cop."

"No duh!" Penny answered with scorn. "I never

would have guessed, what with the uniform and all."

The deputy grabbed her shoulder and stood up. "Come on, you're going with me."

Penny tugged at the hand holding her arm. "No, please. You don't understand. My name's Penny Dixon. I was kidnapped a few weeks ago. I just escaped from this house. Please… the sheriff is in there, and my Uncle Morgan and the guys who kidnapped me and another woman."

The deputy let go her arm and squatted beside her again.

"Wait, you're saying the sheriff kidnapped you? Sheriff Andee Taylor?"

"No, no, no. Sheriff Taylor and my Uncle Morgan and the other woman, Melba Wilson, are being held in the cellar." She rushed to get her words out before the deputy changed his mind and decided to take her back to the house." My uncle shot someone else they call the sheriff. They made him carry the man inside the house, then they shoved us all back down into the cellar. Uncle Morgan got me out of the window before they could block it off. I've been trying to figure out a way to get them out of there, but now there are four of them…"

"Wait. You were kidnapped. Are you one of those gals they kidnapped from the mortuary down in Phoenix?"

Penny nodded her eyes wide. "And now those guys have the sheriff, my uncle and the other woman they kidnapped."

The man stared at Penny for a few seconds. He must have decided she was telling the truth, because he nodded.

"Okay, now, Penny, is it? Have you been in the house? Do you know the layout?"

Penny nodded and with her stick she drew a diagram in the sand. "The cellar stairs come out in the hallway, but the door is locked. The window to the cellar is on this side of the house…" she pointed to the west side of the building. "But they nailed a board on it so no one could get out."

"And you say there are four men in there?"

"Yes. Four."

"I'm going to go call in for back-up. Why don't you come with me. I think you'll be safer if you wait in my truck."

"No," Penny protested, panic in her voice. "Can't you hear that? The sheriff's radio is still on in her truck. If you call for help, they might hear it on her radio." The man hesitated.

"You're right. They might. So what were you planning to do? A little girl all alone out here against four men?"

Penny looked at him with contempt. "Don't

make fun of me. At least I was trying to come up with a plan."

As if making up his mind, the deputy smiled. It was a warm smile. "I'm sorry, Penny. You're right." Penny wrinkled her brow. He seemed sincere.

"I'm Deputy O'Toole. My friends call me Tubby."

Penny almost snickered, and he laughed quietly at her look of sheer disbelief as she stared at his slender, six foot plus frame.

"I know, huh?" he said. "But believe me, when I was in the sixth grade, I was a true Tubby. Kids are cruel. But I outgrew the tubby, just not the name."

He patted her on the shoulder. "I'm not sure what I'm going to do yet. I want you to stay here, out of sight, though, okay. You can watch but stay out of sight. Can you drive?" At her nod, he continued. "If anything happens to me, I want you to run to my Tahoe." He pointed through the trees. "It's just a few yards that direction. You get in it and you drive as fast as you can to St. Johns. When you get to town, call the dispatch. You can say Officer Down, SOS, whatever you want. And then when you get to the Circle K, make a left. You'll come to the sheriff's office about four blocks up. Get into the sheriff's office as fast as you can and finish your story, okay?"

Penny nodded.

"Good girl." He made as if to leave her, and then

turned back. "You aren't going to leave me stranded out here, are you?"

Penny shook her head vigorously. She realized he was teasing as he gave her a grin and a thumbs-up. He crouched down below the thick brush and headed toward the house.

Penny waited until he'd had time to reach the yard before changing her position. Using her makeshift walking stick, she shoved herself into a half standing position. How long would it take before she could actually stand and walk on her own without her legs feeling like rubber, she wondered.

She moved closer to the house. The deputy was almost to the porch. He had just stepped up on the first step when a man backed out through the door, two corners of a makeshift stretcher made from a blanket clutched in his hand.

The deputy jumped back, around the side of the house. It didn't look as if he'd been seen. Penny surmised the burden on the makeshift stretcher was none other than Hilton Parks, the man that her uncle had shot. She held her breath as she watched and waited. She couldn't hear what the men were saying, so she moved a bit closer.

She caught her breath as the fourth man, evidently the back-up guy, came out of the house carrying a gas can. He was pouring the liquid as he advanced. They were going to burn the house with Uncle Morgan, the sheriff and Melba inside. Could one deputy alone stop them?

Using her stick to brace herself, she inched forward through the low brush, keeping her head down as much as possible. She had almost reached the clearing when Deputy O'Toole stepped into view.

"Hold it!" he shouted. "Stop right where you are."

Murphy dropped his burden eliciting curses from Parks as he slid and bumped to the ground. Murphy reached behind him for his weapon, but the deputy pointed his weapon at him, telling him not to try it.

Despite the seriousness of the situation, Penny almost grinned. This was so television-crime-show-script- stuff. What was she thinking? Her whole life for the past few weeks had been television drama.

The man carrying the gas can set it down carefully beside his leg. He casually reached into his pocket withdrawing a book of matches. Penny drew in a breath. Did the deputy see that? The man was half turned away and O'Toole was watching the man with the gun. She had to do something.

The thought had barely left her brain when a shrill sound filled the air around her. She gasped. Not three feet away, a large rattle snake was coiling. Was she far enough away to avoid a strike? She stood perfectly still. If she didn't move… but she couldn't just stand there. Deputy O'Toole had not seen the matches. One little spark and that little house could go up in flames with her Uncle Morgan inside.

She continued to watch the action at the house, while concentrating on the rattlesnake at her feet. Hilton Parks had managed to roll to one side. Penny could see the front of his shirt, stained with blood. It looked like he was still bleeding. She saw his hand inching toward his belt line. Did he still have the gun he'd tried to shoot Morgan with?

O'Toole moved the barrel of his weapon and motioned for the guy with the gas can to move towards the other three men.

"I know you've got weapons," he yelled at them. "Throw them over here, now!"

The men just stood there grinning at him. It was a game of Russian Roulette. O'Toole didn't know if they all had guns, and they knew it. But he wasn't taking any chances.

The snake continued to sing its warning song as Penny watched. Carefully bringing her walking stick up to waist height, she changed ends, putting the forked end toward the ground. There was an off chance her plan wouldn't work. She wasn't sure if she would be able to pull it off. She'd heard of four-year olds who had mimicked things they'd seen on television and saved lives. So why not a seventeen-year old girl? The snake could bite her, but the way she saw it, she might die anyway, so she might as well go down swinging.

Instead of staying together, the men began to move away from each other. There was no way O'Toole could watch them all if they moved far enough apart. *'It's now or never,'* Penny thought as she advanced toward the group of men the deputy was facing off. They had not yet seen her. The sheriff's Tahoe shielded her approach. Ducking down the last few feet, she rounded the Tahoe and stepped into sight of the men.

"I think the Deputy told you to throw out your weapons and stand together," she told them. "And I think you'd best do what he said if you don't want a mad rattler in your midst."

With one hand she held the four foot rattler behind the head and with the other about midway down. As if to clarify her words, she moved her hands upward as if to throw it into the little group.

Hilton Parks cringed on the ground. "What the…" he all but screamed. "Do what she says, boys. Oh crap, I hate snakes." He began to blubber and cry. "Please… just toss those guns out boys. Please. I don't want no snake over here."

Penny raised her arms and threw the snake into their midst. In the scramble to get away from the

angry rattler, they dropped their weapons and proceeded to bring them out from various holding places
and tossed them towards the deputy. Penny looked
back at O'Toole. He was white as a sheet. "Keep an
eye on these guys, deputy," she grinned at him. She
figured the mad rattler would keep the men from
their weapons and allow Deputy O'Toole to keep
them in line.

"Just a minute, I'll get you help." She was up on
the porch and through the front door before the deputy could stop her.

The house reeked with the smell of gas. Penny
knew she was risking her life, but she also knew the
deputy needed help and if things went south, the
house could go up in a blaze within seconds.

She chose the bedroom to enter the hallway. The
key was still in the door.

"Uncle Morgan," she called. Knowing her uncle
he had probably booby trapped the door to the cellar.
She didn't need any surprises. "Uncle Morgan. I've
unlocked the door. Open it."

It opened almost immediately. Morgan stood at
the top of the cellar stairs.

"Penny?"

"You gotta get out of here, quick. There's gas everywhere. They were going to burn the house."

Andee and Melba advanced up the stairs

behind them.

"Penny, you're alright?" Andee wrinkled her nose. "Gas?"

"Yes. Come on. We've got to get out of here. And Deputy O'Toole needs your help."

"O'Toole?" Andee raised her eyebrows.

"I'll explain later. Come on." She all but shoved her uncle and the sheriff out the door towards the men waiting outside. She and Melba followed closely behind.

Chapter 18
Monday, Pre-evacuation
All In A Day's Work

Sheriff Andee and Morgan Freeman arrived back in Round Valley just before six that evening. Andee was exhausted, but it would be a while before she could rest. She and Deputy O'Toole had arrested Hilton Parks and his three men. An ambulance had arrived to take Parks and the women to the hospital, but Melba and Penny had refused to ride in the same ambulance with the man who had kidnapped them. A deputy from the St. Johns district had been dispatched to drive the two women to the hospital in Round Valley. Melba's broken wrist had been x-rayed and set and both women had been admitted to the hospital for observation or until they were no longer in danger of complications from dehydration. Melba's husband was on his way from Gilbert, and

Penny's parents were planning to come for Penny as soon as they could make arrangements for care for their autistic son. Meanwhile, if she was released from the hospital before they arrived, she would stay with Morgan until they did.

The St. Johns fire department was taking care of the potential fire hazard at the Blanton house.

Andee called her dad.

"Hi, Daddy."

"Hey, Sweetie. How's it going?"

Andee swallowed hard. She suddenly felt very vulnerable. The enormity of what had transpired at the Blanton homestead hit her full force. She could have been killed. She could have died from a bullet wound had it not been for her vest. She could have been burned alive, if Tubby O'Toole had not come along; if Penny had not had the guts to capture a rattlesnake.

She shuddered at the thought.

"Are you okay, Andrea?" Her dad always called her Andrea when he thought there was room for concern.

"Yeah, I'm okay Daddy," she told him. "It's just been a rough day." She told him of the day's events, making light of the fact she'd been shot and giving credence to the invention of Kevlar. She left it to his discretion as to telling her mother the whole story.

He laughed with her at the part about Penny and the rattler. "You're right, she's a lot braver than I would be," he laughed. "But on the other hand, I might never kill another rattler, in gratitude for the one who saved my girl's hide."

By this time Andee had settled her nerves and she laughed. "I'm not sure I would go that far, but it was definitely a gutsy thing for Penny to do. She could have been bitten herself, but all she could think of was getting us out of that house before that idiot started a fire.

"I'd better go, Dad. We have pre-evacuation orders in place tonight. My E.T. is in Tucson with a murder victim for autopsy and I've got a disgruntled husband on my hands. Give Mom my love and you guys take care of yourselves. I'll talk to you soon."

Andee gazed out the window of her office. The smoke from the Wallow Fire hung heavy in the air. Bits of soot and burned bark and pine needles floated down from the sky. The night rodeos had been called off since the evacuation of Alpine and Nutrioso. Not many wanted to breathe the ash and smoke-filled air. The livestock had been moved out. Andee was glad about that. It was one more job her office wouldn't have to handle.

Sighing, she hoisted herself out of her desk chair, picked up her briefcase and opened the door.

She had a meeting with Deputy Edison Palmer in fifteen minutes. That was enough time to freshen up and make a pot of coffee if there wasn't already some made.

Edison was right on time. He glanced around the break room when he entered. His eyes settled on Andee.

"You've had a rough day," he stated, concern in his eyes.

Andee sighed and smiled. "You can say that again." She rubbed her chest and winced. Her vest might have protected her from a bullet, but it did nothing to protect the aching bruise beneath it. She had yet to remove the vest to examine the damage. She was almost afraid to know. Seeing it would again bring home to her how close she had come to death today. Twice.

"All in a day's work," Andee laughed. "Nothing like getting shot at and almost burned alive."

"Well, from what I hear, you're the hero today," Edison responded.

"Me? Heck no. Penny's the hero. All the way around. She managed to call her uncle so we'd know where to go looking for her. And then she captured a rattlesnake and threatened the bad guys with it…" she shook her head in disbelief. "That young lady has guts, Ed. Pure and simple. If not for her, there is no telling how the day would have ended."

"They're going to be okay, though? Penny and that Wilson woman?"

Andee nodded. "They'll be fine. Especially now that we've made arrests in the case. Melba's husband is on his way up from Gilbert. Penny will stay with her uncle until her parents can get up here."

"Do you think Parks is responsible for that Montgomery woman's murder?"

"I don't know. We're charging him with it, for now. But it doesn't really fit in with what the girls have told us about their time in captivity. I don't know. We'll have to see."

Talk turned to the reason she and Edison were meeting. Mandatory evacuation of their little town.

Edison showed her a color coded map of the town with sections marked off and names written in. We've notified everyone in the southern end of town from as far west as South Fork and east as far as Picnic Creek. Sipes Wildlife has already been evacuated.

Round Valley was situated in the foothills, right on the edge of the Apache-Sitgreaves National Forest. The forest boundaries came almost to the town limits on the south side. At night, from certain points in the valley, flames could be seen above the tops of the foothills, and an orange glow had permeated the southern sky for several days.

"I think that everything from South Fork to Picnic Creek north of highway 260 will be evacuated tomorrow," Edison told her. "We've knocked on every door and left flyers at every empty residence. We've started notifying the north side. I'm pretty sure they're not far behind"

"Do you have enough manpower to cover the northern part of town tomorrow?"

"We have law enforcement from all over the state," Edison told her. "I'm going to put locals on the evacuation detail. I think they'll be more thorough as they're more familiar with the area."

Andee nodded her approval. "Sounds good, Ed. What do you need me to do?"

Edison grinned and laid his hand on top of her head, much as he had done when she was just a small girl and he'd come to visit her parents.

"Just man the office. You're needed here as much as anywhere." He chuckled. "Besides, I hear you're supposed to be getting a call from a lawyer pretty soon. Something about a husband wanting his wife's body released, or else?"

Andee's eyes opened wide. "Oh my gosh! Do I have a mole in the office? Everyone seems to know everything about anything these days."

"I was in the jail area when Sandra came to give O.P. a heads up about the guy," he explained. "Go home. Get some rest. I'll see you tomorrow."

———◈———

Andee climbed the steps to her little house on the hill. She had always dreamed of a house on top of Graveyard Hill. Not Graveyard Hill exactly, as that part of the dyke that divided the town was just that, a grave yard. But to the south, it was private land with several houses breaking the skyline from either side. She had bought there for the view.

To the north, lay one of the largest extinct volcanic fields in North America. To the south, the Apache-Sitgreaves National Forest, foothills and the largest Ponderosa Pine forest in the world, or at least it was until now, and this destructive Wallow Fire, which had to date, burned over 233,552 acres. *"So sad,"* she thought.

On the east, before the valley ended and climbed up the surrounding mountains, was farmland, or what was left of it. So many farms were gone, giving way to the drought that had plagued the area for more than 25 years. New construction had taken over these fields of alfalfa hay and winter oats. But it was the view to the west that always caught her eye and gave her a sense of peace. Antelope Mountain, Green's Peak, and the mountains beyond stretched before her eyes. At any given time of the day and with the passing of each season, the view was ever changing. Sometimes the distant mountains took on a deep purple, while the nearer ones, like Antelope Mountain and Green's Peak were a rich golden brown until giving away to the dark blue-green of the nearer mountains. In the winter they were brushed with snow, and sometimes the storms hid them from view. During monsoon they lay lush and green.

Tonight, gray smoke covered the entire valley, almost obscuring the mountains beyond. The sun had set and the last vestiges of light filtered through the hazy smoke. She longed to sit in the glider chair on the front porch and relax before retiring for the day, but she knew it would be foolish to breathe any more smoke. The health department had already warned about the pollution levels.

Sighing, she turned and unlocked the front door. Securing it behind her, she turned down the hallway towards her bedroom and the bathroom. Hanging her sidearm and holster over a hook on the door, she pulled the Velcro tabs on her vest and eased it over her head. Part of it bumped her chest as she removed it and she winced. Dropping the vest on the bed, she gingerly explored the soreness under her shirt, and then lifted the tail to expose the area. It was not pretty.

It's a wonder the bullet hadn't broken her rib. Her skin was deep blue around the area of impact, just under her left breast, with angry red flowing from the center outward. She placed her hand over the bruise and bits of it peeked from under her fingers. She knew it would move downward as gravity did its job. It wasn't going to get prettier for a while.

Leaving her bedroom, she retraced her steps down the hallway to the kitchen. Pulling open a cupboard door she pulled out a small, zippered baggie and filled it with ice from the freezer. She debated on whether she should make herself a light supper or not, and decided she would skip it for the night. She was just too tired.

Back in the bedroom, she turned on the shower, undressed and stood beneath the warm spray. Thoughts raced through her mind as she recalled the events of the day. Despite her earlier distrust, Morgan had proven to be a worthy back-up. She didn't know what the outcome would have been had he not been there with them. After splinting her wrist, Melba had fainted on them. Morgan had picked her up and put her on the bed. When she came to, he encouraged her to drink some water and assured her that Penny would be fine.

She'd told them a bit about their ordeal. About

being kidnapped and being moved several times before being left alone in the cellar of the old homestead. She told them how she and Penny had worked to get the little window open so Penny could get out of it. It had been nailed shut, but they had found a butter knife under the bed and gradually pried the window open.

"I wouldn't let Penny go through the window until we'd removed all the nails," Melba said. "I was afraid they would do her more harm if she hit one of them, so I used the sole of my shoe to pound them through the wood to the other side."

"And then she came back," Melba had exclaimed. "I told her to send help. I didn't want her to come back here, but bless her; she was afraid of what they would do to me if they came back and found her gone." She smiled wanly. "A lot of good it did her to come back. They didn't even know she had left and they decided to leave us and let us die in this house."

She said that she heard Murphy talking and he said the sheriff (Parks) had told him about finding Roma Montgomery dead up in the mountains so he and his son were taking a vacation in Canada, and the rest of them could do what they wanted.

Morgan had headed up the cellar stairs to try and listen in on whatever plans the former sheriff and his men were making, when he smelled the gas fumes.

He was debating on whether to try and break the door down or try and jimmy the lock when Penny turned the key and called through the door at him.

⸺»«⟨●⟩»«⸺

Andee rinsed the shampoo from her hair. It even hurt to raise her hands above her head. It was not going to be a comfortable night.

She wrapped a towel around her head and dried with a large, luxurious, fluffy bath towel. It was a gift from her mother that was way out of her budget. Donning pajamas, she quickly shook out her hair and combed it. Wrapping the bag of ice she had prepared, in a towel, she slipped it under her pajama top, swallowed two pain killers and crawled into bed.

She thought she would lie awake most of the night, her mind was so busy, but she was asleep almost before she'd found a comfortable position to lie in. However, her dreams were not restful. She was locked in slow motion as Hilton Parks leveled his 9mm at her and fired. She watched as the bullet left the barrel of his gun and traveled slowly through the air towards her. She tried to move, to dodge the bullet, but as she watched it move towards her it became larger and there was no escaping. She cried out as it

— 203 —

hit her, then she was falling and falling and falling, oh why couldn't she wake up? She always woke up in her falling dreams. Suddenly a pair of strong arms caught her and held her tight, pulling her up against a solid chest. At first she thought it was her dad. Didn't he always come through for her? Didn't he always save her? She caught her breath as she looked into the clear blue eyes of Morgan Freeman. He was laughing. She screamed at him to let her down, but he laughed and held her tighter. "I can't put you down," he told her, and he laughed again. "I saved you. Now you're mine!"

The ringing of the phone awakened her. A quick glance at the lighted dial on the clock beside her bed told her she'd been asleep less than an hour.

"Sheriff Taylor."

"Andee, did I wake you?" If she had not just been dreaming about him in that ridiculous dream…

"Actually, you did," she all but snarled. "I'm really tired, Morgan. What do you want?"

"I just wanted to let you know that Penny's dad showed up at the hospital. My sister stayed with their son, Evan. Don came to get Penny. They'll be leaving in the morning as soon as she's discharged. She wanted to say goodbye before she left. I thought maybe we could get breakfast."

She wanted to be snarly again. The image of his

blue eyes and laughing mouth and hard secure chest sent sensations through her body she didn't want to think about, but there was also a kind of reassurance, knowing that even in her dreams he had her back.

"Okay, sure. What time?"

"Well, you're better acquainted with the doctors and their schedules than I am. What time do you think they'll release her?"

She smiled. "Beats me. I've got a couple of things I need to do at the office in the morning. Why don't you call me when she's discharged and I'll meet you at the Mill?

"Just remember if it's after eleven, it'll have to be lunch," she admonished.

They agreed, but just before he hung up, Morgan asked, "Andee. Are you doing alright? You sounded kind of out of sorts when you answered the phone."

"I'm fine. I was just reliving the events of the day in my dreams and I had no control, so they weren't going quite like it happened. I'm going to fix myself a cup of tea to help me relax and sleep. I'll be fine. And Morgan, thanks for asking."

Chapter 19
Tuesday, June 7, 2011

Is My Tower Gone?

In the break room the next morning Edison Palmer reported that there had been little going on in town the night before, and that evacuation of the southern part of Round Valley was inevitable.

"Probably sometime after noon today," he told her. "Your folks already left?"

Andee nodded.

"That's good. I sent Bethany with her mom and Colin over to my brother's in Heber. He has a dog and some horses. Only two weeks out of school and Colin was getting bored at home." He shook his head. "I guess I should be grateful he is not into staying home and playing video games. He just wanted to play baseball, but I didn't think it was a good idea for him to be out in this smoke too much."

"I think that's wise," Andee told him. "What was that they said on the news yesterday? Two hundred ninety-five particulates per…? How do they measure that? Anyway, the healthy air quality was 26 in Flagstaff and Prescott. So however they measure it, one can do the math and see it's not healthy being out in it. Especially if you're a kid or asthmatic. That's why the folks left. Mom was having a hard time breathing."

They chatted a while longer about the effects of the fire on the town. Edison finished his coffee and washed out his cup. "I'm going to hit the hay for a few hours. They're going to call me if they start the evacuation before noon."

"How long have you been out?" she asked him.

"I caught a few hours sleep Saturday night and an hour or two Sunday morning," he told her. "I'll catch four hours this morning; I'll be good as new."

Andee shook her head.

"Get some rest."

It was almost ten before Morgan called to tell her Penny had been released.

"Penny really wants some of those biscuits and gravy I've been telling her about," he told Andee. "Do you think you could pull some weight and get them to keep the breakfast menu open for us?"

Andee laughed. "What am I? A miracle worker?"

she asked. "Listen, if we hurry, there'll be no need for intervention. They serve breakfast until eleven o'clock. I'll meet you there in ten minutes. Order me orange juice and coffee if I'm late."

She hung up with Morgan and dialed the hospital number. They were keeping Melba for another day. They put her through and she talked briefly with the older woman. "I'm sending someone over to get your statement sometime today. You probably can't write with that wrist broken, so I'm sending someone who can write it down and all you'll have to do is sign it."

Melba told her once again how grateful she was to have been rescued at last, and assured Andee she'd try and remember everything from the time she was kidnapped on.

"As much as you can," Andee told her. "But don't upset yourself. If you forget anything, you can amend it later."

She said goodbye to Melba and called the mortuary. She wanted to give Bruce a heads-up that Roger Montgomery would be in to make arrangements. As it turned out, Montgomery was already at the mortuary. He'd been waiting when Bruce and his receptionist arrived to open up.

Andee hung up with Bruce and locked up her office. After telling Sandra where she would be, she started the Tahoe and drove to the Sawmill Restaurant.

The smoke was heavy in the air this morning, but the usual mix of coffee drinkers and breakfast patrons were at the restaurant. Andee was hailed several times and stopped to talk as she made her way to the group sitting in a corner booth. The talk, of course, was mostly about the fire and whether there had been any progress in controlling it.

"Everyone south of State Route 260 will probably be evacuated today," Andee told the men at one table.

"I'm not leaving," one elderly man spouted. "It's my home and they can't force me to leave."

Andee smiled. "You can do as you wish Mr. Kinser. If you elect to stay, you *will* be required to stay on your property. They reported it had burned over 311,000 acres this morning. My calculations make that over 77,000 acres since yesterday."

She left the men talking about the fire and managed to make it to the party in the corner before stopping again. Hugging Penny she sat down beside her. Penny introduced her to the man sitting beside her. "This is my dad, Don Dixon," she said proudly, hugging his arm.

Andee acknowledged Dixon, and waved aside his praise and gratitude for rescuing his daughter.

"If it hadn't been for Morgan and Penny's heroic actions with that rattlesnake, I doubt you'd be seeing any of us here," she told him. And then addressing Penny, she said, "You look none the worse for wear. Can we start calling you the rattlesnake wrangler? You know the newspaper is going to want a story from you. You can downplay it if you want, but I, my dear, am going to tell them all about it."

"Do you think I'll make front page?" Penny asked. "I always wanted to see my face plastered on the front page of a newspaper." She frowned and smiled impishly. "Maybe not with the fire going on and all. Do you think they'd wait till the fire is under control so I could get full glory?"

They all laughed and her dad jokingly reprimanded her.

After the meal, they bid farewell to the Dixons.

"Now you can crash," Andee told Morgan. "It's over and she's safe."

Morgan grinned wryly. "I would do just that if I didn't have stock to feed and two other cases to look into."

Andee raised an eyebrow. "Anything I should know about?" She punched him on the shoulder and winced as pain shot through her chest at the effort.

It was Morgan's turn to raise an eyebrow. "I'll let you know," he said. "Did you go to the hospital and have that bruise looked at?"

"I'm good," she told him. "I slept with an ice pack last night. It's better today."

"Which is your way of avoiding a direct answer to my question," he said sternly. "Are you going to get it looked at or not?"

"Not. I've got too much work to do. Besides, there is nothing they can do for it."

"What if it broke a rib?" he demanded.

"What if it did? I repeat, *Mr. Freestone*, there is nothing the doctors could do about it. I can wrap my ribs if I think I need it. I can icepack the bruise. Thanks for your concern, but I've got this, okay?"

She walked briskly to her Tahoe and clicked the button to unlock the door. With a curt nod of her head, she climbed into the seat and backed out of the parking lot. When she looked back Morgan was standing where she had left him. She could see the frown on his face as he gazed after her.

By three o'clock Tuesday afternoon mandatory evacuations were in place. Newscasts informed the residents living south of Highway 260 and Central Avenue, the residential area nearest the oncoming fire, to leave as soon as possible. Law enforcement issued two strips of colored tapes to each resident. One was tied to the fence or a tree to indicate that the residence had been notified, the other was given to the homeowner to place next to the other one when they left the residence.

Amy Holland carried the last box of personal belongings to her vehicle. It wasn't hard packing up what was important. She had a laptop computer, a few pictures, her clothes and Belou, her cat. She wore a wet kerchief over her mouth and nose, but she coughed anyway. She really didn't want to evacuate. Since her harrowing ride off the mountain, the night John Wilson's crew had awakened her, she'd been depressed. She knew, without a doubt, her lookout tower was gone. She envisioned it in her dreams. Sometime the flames licked at it teasingly, and it stood staunch and sturdy, but at others her dreams were filled with her flying trip off the mountain, and then she would stand and watch as flames engulfed the tower and ash from the old wood drifted to the ground below. She couldn't think about it without crying. Maybe it was silly. It was just a structure. John, so practical all the time, would probably think so, but she couldn't help it.

There was a lot of history in that tower. Thankfully she'd grabbed the satchel that contained her book of notes on it; stuff she'd gathered since the first year she worked there. She had realized then that the tower held history and had started to write it down. She devoured the information, processed it and knew that one day she would not only write about its history, but weave a book of fiction from events that had taken place there.

But now she was unemployed. Heck, if this fire advanced much further she could actually be homeless in a matter of minutes. If she didn't find a job to pay the rent, she'd be homeless anyway. She smiled inwardly. Worse things had happened. At least she was alive. She had Belou. She had John, or did she? Just because he hung out at the tower now and then, just because he always seemed to smile at her in a special way, just because they had dated once when they were both off duty, just because she wanted it, didn't make it so.

She climbed into the old Dodge truck she'd acquired from her younger brother when he left for the military and turned the key in the ignition. The old familiar grinding from the starter filled her ears and she pounded the steering wheel. She tried again and again to no avail. Tears of frustration filled her eyes. No job, no ride, soon to be no home; depression assailed her again.

Grabbing the cat carrier, she took Belou and unlocked the trailer door. Law enforcement had given her blue tape to tie to the door when she left. She removed it and stuffed it in her purse.

She found the phone book in the shelf under the

phone, but sat and stared at it for a full minute before opening it to the yellow pages. She had no idea who to call. Her older brother had always done her mechanic work, but he had moved to Denver the year before. Did she need someone to tow the truck or a mechanic to fix it? Was there anyone left in the town to do the work, anyway? Either way, it needed to be fixed. She found two numbers and wrote them down. Dragging the phone to her lap, she dialed the first one. After six rings, the answering machine picked up, informing callers that the owner had taken his family to a safe place and would return as soon as they were settled.

She signed in frustration and dialed the next number, but before it began to ring on the other end, there was a pounding on her door.

"Amy, it's John, open up."

She unlocked the door and stood looking up at the ruggedly handsome face of John Wilson. Again tears filled her eyes. She just stood there as they dripped down her face. A look of concern passed over his face. Suddenly she was caught up in an embrace so smothering she had to wiggle her face from his broad chest to breathe.

"Oh, Honey, I was so worried. Are you okay?"

She shook her head and gave a little giggle. Pulling away, she stared up into John's kind and concerned face.

"No. Is it gone, John? Is my tower gone?" At his stricken nod in the affirmative, an emptiness filled her and she began to babble about losing the tower and her job, about being broke and having no place to go, and then last about her truck not starting and not knowing who to call. "I'm such a mess, John. You'd think as long as I've lived alone I'd be independent and would know everything, but I'm just a helpless bowl of jelly and I can't even think straight."

John laughed, but it was a kind laugh.

"So Oscar finally died on you, huh?" Oscar was what she called the old Dodge pick-up truck she owned. She'd named it, as a joke, after her little brother, whose middle was Oscar.

John gave her orders to sit tight and left her to go check the truck. She watched him through the window. He had shaved since she'd seen him last. He was wearing a red plaid shirt and blue jeans. She smiled and her heart skipped a beat. John Wilson cleaned up pretty darned good.

He raised the hood of the truck and fiddled with something underneath. He went to his own truck and removed a toolbox, extracted a tool and once more bent under the hood of Oscar. Fifteen minutes later he climbed the two steps to her trailer door and stepped inside. He was holding the faulty starter.

"I'll just run down and get a replacement and we'll have you going in no time," he smiled reassuringly.

"I need to go with you." She grabbed her purse and made to follow him out the door.

"I've got it," John argued. "You stay with Belou. You don't need to be breathing any more of this smoke.

Amy blushed. "John," she stammered. "I don't have the money. I need to charge it on my card."

Holding the starter mid-air in one hand, John grabbed her around the shoulders with his other arm and hugged her to his chest. Kissing the top of her head, he whispered, "I told you, I've got this." When she would have protested more, he simply turned her towards the kitchen and told her, "Make us something to eat while I'm gone."

He was gone before she had made it across the floor to the little kitchen alcove. Something to eat, huh? Tears threatened again and she dashed them away. She had already turned off the propane, so it would have to be a cold something. She opened the pantry cupboard and searched its contents. She had cans of tuna, potted meat and spam. Spam seemed the best bet. She hurried about making sandwiches. She had to go out to her truck to haul in a box of things she'd packed to take with her from her refrigerator, but by the time John had returned she had a nice little lunch prepared.

Less than an hour later, the new starter was installed and Oscar was running like a top. They sat across from each other in her little dining nook. Neither said much as they munched spam sandwiches and drank water. Amy was afraid to say much for fear she would start blubbering again. John's mind seemed far away.

Amy finished first and began clearing the paper plates away from the table. She wiped crumbs from her place, and tossed the plate in the trash. She carried her glass to the sink and ran a couple of inches of hot water in the bottom. John suddenly appeared behind her, placing his water glass in the sink beside hers, his arms encircled her waist.

He nuzzled her hair and cleared his throat.

"Amy."

She stiffened. This behavior was totally not John. There had always been an attraction between them, but they had always kept their relationship impersonal. Even on the one date they shared, John had not kissed her, or even held her hand, for that matter. Oh, she'd dreamed about it. She'd dreamed about it plenty.

He turned her to face him. "You know, I really like you a lot," John smiled down at her.

"You do?"

"I do. We've been really good friends, but lately I've been thinking about you in a rather more friendly way. You know what I mean?"

It was Amy's turn to smile. She nodded. "I think I do."

He pulled her closer and bent his head. He brushed her lips in their first kiss. Amy's arms curled around his neck and she responded to his kiss, shyly at first, then with abandon and commitment.

John was the first to pull away. He drew a deep breath and shook his head. He dropped his arms and pulled away from her.

"You nearly scared me to death the other night," he admonished her. "When they said the fire was headed for Big Lake and the dispatcher told me you were staying at the tower, all I could think of was what if I lost you?" He moved and paced the floor of her living room. He ran his hands through his hair. "Driving up there, trying to beat the monster… I nearly went crazy." He returned to stand in front of her; he pulled her back into his arms. "Maybe it's a little early to say I love you, I don't want to scare you away, but that night…thinking we might not get to you in time, I think a little part of me died. Sweetheart, I can't imagine my life without you."

Amy placed both her hands on his arms and rose on her tip toes to brush his lips in a reassuring kiss.

"I don't think it's too early. I think I started falling in love with you the first time you climbed the steps into my tower. Your presence just seemed to fill the room with comfort. And then the rest of your crew came in..."

John laughed. "And really filled the room. All five of us!"

Chapter 20
Wednesday, June 8, 2011
She's Gone Forever

Frank Rosencrans stared out the window of his posh Peoria home. She was gone. Roma was gone. They'd found her body in the mountains. He would never see her again. He wasn't a crying man. He was a mortician for Pete's sake. He dealt with death on a daily basis. He always remained steady and strong, even in the face of a family's most moving grief. But this was Roma. This was his love.

Despite himself, tears trickled down his cheeks. He dashed them away, but more followed. He had loved her from the moment he saw her. She was such a nervous, timid creature when she answered his ad for a receptionist/secretary at the mortuary. He'd hired her on the spot and she had gone to work for him the next day. When his apprentice helper moved on he had not hired a new one. He wanted Roma all to himself. She had easily moved into the spot as helper. She helped him dress and casket. He'd taught her makeup and she could do wonders with hair. They worked well together. Now she was gone. Forever.

She hadn't loved that worthless husband of hers. Too many times she had come to work wearing sun glasses and long sleeves and high necked blouses, trying to cover the bruises he had left on her during one of his rages. He'd even put her in the hospital once. Yet she remained loyal to him. Or maybe it was just fear that kept her there.

He knew he would have treated her like a queen if only she would have agreed to leave Roger and go with him. He'd have risked everything just to have her by his side. They could have moved out of state and started a new life. He would have loved her kids as his own.

Now there was no chance of that ever happening. Roma was gone. Dead. Murdered. He clinched his fist. He just wanted to hit something.

He heard Frankie coming down the stairs behind him. He stiffened. He didn't feel like a fight this morning. He just wanted to wallow in his grief without his wife's constant interference. He placed a slight smile on his face and turned to greet her.

"I thought you'd be gone by now," she said before he could utter a word. "But since you're still here, do you want me to place an ad for a new receptionist?"

Frank grimaced, then quickly straightened his face.

"What?" she questioned. "You know you're going to need someone. You can't handle everything alone. Besides, Roma is dead. It's not like she's on vacation and will be back in a week or so."

"You're cold, Frankie. She's not even in her grave yet and you're already wanting me to replace her. Give it a rest." He turned and headed for the front door. Grabbing his keys from the bowl in the foyer, he reached for the handle on the double doors that led to their spacious front porch.

"Don't you walk away from me!" Frankie shouted at him. "For once, why can't you be a man and finish a conversation? If you think I'm going to step in and help you, you've got another think coming. You know I hate that place."

"I don't need your help, Frankie. I'll take care of the business myself. Just like I've always done."

His wife, Frances Elizabeth Helen Smith Rosencrans had been a nobody when they started dating. Unlike his family, who lived in luxury, she came from the poorer side of town. Frank hadn't cared. She was beautiful and fun to be around. He hadn't loved her, but she fit in with his family and friends and they had gotten along well, so when his family started pressuring him to get married and start a family, he had asked her to marry him.

Everyone had always called her Frankie, so when they had started dating, it had been cute that they were Frank and Frankie. Then later when they married, they joked about having to be careful of opening each other's mail. They'd been happy that first couple of years. That is, until Frank realized the hardware business was not what he wanted to do with his life. When he had chosen a career as a funeral director and mortician, Frankie had gone ballistic. Frankie was a snob. She'd looked forward to being the wife of a hardware king. His family owned a hardware chain that covered most of the east coast and gulf coast states. He was destined to become the CEO of that business making six figures a year. Frankie visualized herself as the wife of the king. Vacations in Europe and South America, jewelry, fancy cars, and a million dollar house, all while she headed up her charity work for various foundations and causes.

She'd almost divorced him when he'd told her he was leaving the family business and the career choice he had made. Now, he wished she had, but he had convinced her to stay, telling her he would make a lot of money as a mortician. Maybe not as much as

CEO of a successful hardware chain, but enough that they could live in the upper tax bracket comfortably. She could still head up her charities. He promised she would not want for money as a mortician's wife.

In retrospect he wished he knew then what he knew now. Life would have been so much simpler if only he had just let her go. If he'd not been married, maybe Roma would have been more willing to leave Roger. Roma was like that. Very moral. She believed marriage was until death. But maybe... He shook himself mentally. It did no good to fantasize about what might have been now. Now it would never be. He had loved her. And now he had lost her forever.

"I'll see you tonight," he said to his wife, and then under his breath he muttered, "maybe." He wanted to slam the door when he left, but he knew it would please her to know she had gotten to him again. He closed it gently to spite her and then kicked the huge potted fern that graced the steps. Before his foot connected with the large terra cotta clay pot he knew it was a mistake, but he couldn't stop the momentum of the kick.

Sharp pain shot up his foot and into his ankle. He swore and set his foot gingerly down on the porch. *"Stupid, stupid, stupid,"* he chided himself.

He grasped the white column near the steps and forced himself to put weight on the injured foot. He bit his lip and continued to his car. He pushed the remote that unlocked his door and fell into the low seat of his black Corvette. He knew as he dropped he had not compensated for the low roof and hot on the thought he felt the searing pain at the back of his head as he connected with the roof over the door.

He placed his hand over the back of his head and felt the warm sticky flow of blood between his fingers. He swore again and lifted his injured foot into the car. If he could just make it to the office, he would take care of both injuries.

━━━●━━━

Wednesday, June 8, just eleven days after the Wallow fire began, everyone north of Highway 260 had been ordered to evacuate. By nightfall, the streets were empty except for an occasional business owner, with permits to stay, or an emergency vehicle. Over 336,187 acres had been burned. Arizona was in the headlines daily. The Wallow Fire was being held back at both Alpine and Nutrioso. Some outlying buildings and residences had been consumed. Containment was still zero percent.

Andee had scheduled patrols to cover the whole town, watching for spot fires and possible vandalisms.

Penny and her father had gone home directly after breakfast the morning before. Melba Webster had been released earlier this morning and was anxious to return to Gilbert to her only grandchild.

The body of Roma Montgomery had been released and was on the way to the crematory. Roger Montgomery had visited her office one last time, making demands about finding her killer, before he returned to Peoria to make funeral arrangements for his wife.

Andee drove down the deserted streets, keeping a watchful eye for anything suspicious. Her cell phone rang and she pulled to the side of the road to take the call.

"Hi, Mom. How are you?"

"Oh Andee, are you okay? I just read the paper. You were shot? Oh, Honey, you were shot!"

"Mom, I was wearing a vest. I'm okay. Just bruised."

"But Hilton Parks shot you? I knew that man was no good. I can't believe he was the sheriff for so long. Honey, do you need anything? Your dad can be there in a couple of hours."

"No, Mom," she assured her mother. "I'm fine. Everything is fine. The entire town has been evacuated. There's no need for Daddy to come back over here. You guys just enjoy your little holiday."

"But if you need anything, if you need us, you'll call, won't you?"

"Yes, I'll call. I promise. I love you. Give Daddy my love, too."

She hung up and smiled. Her dad was probably kicking himself for not hiding the paper from her mom. Her smile turned to chuckle. Her mom was probably kicking him for not telling her their daughter had been held hostage and shot. That would keep them occupied for a few hours. She could almost hear their bickering. They never got angry, but they bickered about silly things, and sometimes serious things.

Andee pulled back onto the roadway and continued her patrol of the town. Her thoughts stayed on her mom and dad as she drove. They'd been married thirty-five years and still acted like love-birds most of the time. She remembered as a teenager how she and her sister, Jean, had been embarrassed by the entire hand holding and kissing thing they had done, but as they had matured they realized what a wonderful thing their parents had together.

That was one of the reasons Andee had never committed to anyone. There had been a few boy-friends while she was in college, but noone serious. Maybe her standards were just too high. Some of her girlfriends thought so, but Andee knew she would never be satisfied in a relationship with anything less than what her mom and dad had together.

An image of Morgan Freeman flashed through her mind. Tall, dark and handsome. Handsome? He was over-the-top good looking with blue eyes rimmed with dark lashes that any girl would die to have. Andee shook her head, trying to clear the image of unruly curls and blue eyes from her mind.

What was the matter with her? She'd only known Morgan for a few short days. Although one of those days had lasted what seemed like twenty, and he had more than passed the test as reliable. His niece, Penny, and his brother-in-law seemed to think he was right up there in the hero department.

She was glad he had been with her when they went to check out the old Blanton farm. Things could have ended a lot differently had he not been there.

Her mind wandered to the events since Memorial Day. The Wallow Fire alone was enough to keep her office busy, but having two kidnappings, a murder and the arrest of the former sheriff and his cronies at the Blanton place just added up to complicate things further.

Parks was being charged with the murder of Roma Montgomery, but something didn't set right with that particular case. Her mind ran back over what Morgan had told her about the last kidnapping. In the previous two cases, Melba Wilson and Penny

Dixon, the kidnappers had left the more recent death files and broken into storage for the older ones. They had held the women and moved them several times before abandoning them at the Blanton place. It was after news that the sheriff's office had found a body, a possible murder victim, that Parks and his men had decided to abandon Penny and Melba.

Blood was found at the mortuary where Roma Montgomery was taken; blood that matched that of the victim. Was it a kidnapping gone wrong, or was it a copy-cat murder following the MO of the other victims to throw the police off? If that was the case, the murderer had not followed the previous kidnappings to a tee. Something wasn't right.

Andee made a U-turn and headed back to her office.

She dialed Morgan's number and tapped her fingers on her desk as she waited for him to answer. When he didn't pick up, she left a brief message for him to call her and hung up.

She unlocked her file cabinet and extracted the file she had copied from Morgan's case files. Leafing through pages she grabbed a packet of sticky notes and began jotting things down as she read. As she read the last page of the report, she reached for the button on her computer and turned it on. She needed to read the newspaper reports. Something didn't gel.

Before her computer had completely booted, her desk phone buzzed. Sandra told her Morgan was returning her call. "Mr. Freeman," Andee answered.

Morgan chuckled. "After all we've been through together, don't you think we can drop the formalities, And-re-ra?" He drawled her full name.

Her mouth twitched. "Maybe."

"So what's up? I know it has to be important for you to call me."

Andee told him she was going over the kidnapping case files. "I was just going to read the online news stories about the kidnappings. But maybe you can tell me. How much information did the police release in the kidnapping case. Was the information about case files released as a motive?" While she talked she was pulling up the newspaper accounts of the case.

"I have them now," she told him. "Hold on." She quickly scanned the page. Nothing about files being stolen. She brought up the next page and the next.

"Do you know why that information was held back?" she asked him.

"Not really. I think there was so little evidence; they may have decided to keep some of their eggs in the basket."

"So, when Penny and Melba were taken, they broke into a storage room and took several boxes of case files. But when Roma was taken, only recent files were taken."

"You're thinking, like me, different perps, only half the MO?"

"But if Parks didn't take Roma," Andee said, "how did the perp know to take any files at all, if that part of the crime wasn't released to the newspapers? Do you think the individual mortuary owners discussed the crimes among themselves? Do you think Roma might have mentioned the stolen files to anyone? Her husband? I need to make some phone calls. Do you have numbers for the mortuaries where all these women worked?"

She jotted the numbers down and thanked him for his help.

Two hours later Andee had talked to the proprietors of all three mortuaries from which the women had been taken. The first two kidnappings were much as her information from Morgan stated. The women had been alone in the mortuary. There were no prints, no blood, but damage to storage area and several boxes of old files taken. The third was similar, except there were signs of struggle, blood on the floor and the door handle, and no break-in to storage areas. Only current files, or files from this year were taken.

Melba would not be home yet. She dialed the

Dixon's number. It was Penny who answered. After a brief conversation, and a few more jotted notes, she hung up and chewed the end of her pen. It just didn't add up.

Reaching for her index file, she looked up the number for the Gilbert Police Department, called and asked to speak to the detective in charge of the Wilson kidnapping. Detective Silvia Raymond responded to her call. Raymond knew the women had been found in Apache County and was waiting for both women to arrive back in the valley before questioning them.

"How far apart are the three mortuaries?" Andee asked.

"Bethel and Montrose are about a mile apart," Detective Raymond told her. "Montrose is in Gilbert. Bethel just over in Chandler. Rosencrans is in north Peoria. That's across the city. Maybe twenty miles."

"When I questioned the women here, they said that until they were thrown together in the back of a van, they had never set eyes on one another. Nor did they know the Montgomery woman. I'm trying to find a connection to the kidnappings and the murder and things just aren't adding up. If the same people took Montgomery that took the other women, why didn't they take the same kind of files from that mortuary? And why kill her? Melba Wilson said she put up one heck of a fight, and Penny Dixon said she kicked and screamed until they tied her up and stuffed a gag in her mouth. Was Montgomery's death an accident? What's Montgomery's connection? If there is one."

"You don't think your former sheriff was involved in all three?" the detective asked her.

"I wish I could say I've solved all three crimes," Andee said. "But Parks wasn't a murderer. Well, not at the time of the kidnappings. It wasn't until we found the body of Roma Montgomery that things went south for him. Wilson and Dixon heard him talking to one of his flunkies. He told them there had been a body found and he wasn't sticking around to face a murder charge along with the kidnapping."

"But didn't he try to kill you?"

Andee smiled wryly. "Yeah. He did. All of us. Still, I'm not sure he is responsible for the murder of Roma Montgomery."

"I'm following a couple of leads down here," the detective told her. "If anything pans out, I'll call you."

Andee thanked her and hung up.

Whoever had killed Roma Montgomery and hidden her body had taken a big chance, bringing it all the way from the Phoenix area. If it wasn't Parks, why would the body be in the same general area that they found the other women? If it hadn't been for a raging wildfire, would anyone have found her before all evidence was gone? It was just a fluke that those firefighters were looking for a better vantage point to start some back burning. Whoever had dumped the body had chosen the spot well. It was off the beaten path. A four wheel drive was about the only type of vehicle that could manage that road. If the engine crew hadn't had to stop to remove rocks from the road, the body may well have gone undiscovered for years. Or maybe never.

She pulled the autopsy report from the Montgomery file. Cause of death, asphyxiation. But she also had been stabbed. The stab wound would have eventually caused her death. She would have bled out, given time. Maybe the murderer didn't have the time to wait. How convenient that the mortuary had heavy duty body bags. The blood at the scene of the original crime was minimal, according to the Peoria police. A bit on the floor, and some on the inside door handle to the back door. A couple of drops on the cement on garage floor outside.

She called Carlie. "Anything on that handle thing we found at the dump scene?"

"I was just going to call you," Carlie laughed. "We got a partial print. We got some prints off the body bag, too. Not sure if it's enough to get a match. We're running them though all the databases now. The lab will let me know if anything comes up. I found a button when I examined the body. It was under her in the body bag. We got a partial off it. Whoever left the button probably lost it when he zipped her into that bag. We found a couple of hairs, but they may belong to the vic. It's not much to go on. I think fingerprints are the best we have to go on now, unless we can get an eyewitness, which isn't likely, considering where the body was found."

They hung up and Andee went back to her notes and files.

At noon she locked up her office and called to Sandra that she was going to get some lunch. She met Bernie in the parking lot.

"Anything new?" Andee asked.

"Nope. I was just coming to see if you wanted to eat some lunch." She indicated a box in the back seat of her Tahoe. "My mom and dad evacuated this morning, but not before Mom cooked enough food for the entire town. I have tamales, enchiladas, the makings for tacos, some guacamole and some salsa. My refrigerator is not big enough to hold all this so I thought we could go to your place to eat and then unload the leftovers into your fridge."

Andee laughed. "I just happen to have some cherry pie that my mom baked before she left. Let's do it."

They drove the short distance to Andee's house overlooking the western side of the valley and the mountains. The mountains could hardly be seen because the smoke. They carried the box of food inside shutting the door against the heat and the smoke outside. In the kitchen Andee switched on the light. Even with the skylight over head, there was little light filtering through.

Andee set out paper plates and plastic cups, while Bernie heated enchiladas and tamales in the microwave.

"Soda, iced tea, water or coffee?" she asked Bernie.

"I'd better go with water," Bernie answered. "I'm parched. This smoke is killing my throat."

They ate in companionable silence until their appetites where sated. Talk automatically turned to the business at hand.

"Any containment on the fire?" Bernie asked.

Andee shook her head sadly. "Not yet. This morning's count was over 336,000 acres."

"How's that going to affect our tourism? Will that put a halt to the Chamber's plans for summer activities?"

"I'm sure it will. I doubt we'll be allowed back into the forest for a while. If there is anything left to go to. The nightly rodeo, the carnival and the street vendors are good pulls, but without the camping and fishing, who knows? I guess we'll see how it goes when it's over."

"Changing the subject a little," Bernie said," but do you think Hilton Parks really kidnapped that Montgomery woman and killed her?"

Andee shook her head. "I want to say he did, but there are just too many factors in the case that say he didn't. For one thing, it's too messy. Blood, prints and files taken."

"You got prints?"

"Yeah. Carlie said they got a partial off the handle thing and a button she found under the body in the body bag. Also some on the body bag. They're running the prints at the lab. I talked to the detective on the Webster case, in Gilbert. She's working with Chandler PD on the Dixon case since the two are obviously related. She asked me if I thought Parks was good for the Montgomery case, but I'm just not sure."

"Well," Bernie said. "I'd like to hang him for the entire package."

"Bernadette!" Andee admonished.

"Well, I would. He tried to kill you, for gosh sakes! That right there says he is capable of murder. And he was going to allow his flunkies to burn the house down around your ears! Good grief, Andee! Go for it!"

She grinned. "Okay. If Parks isn't guilty of Montgomery's murder, and he is convicted, then the real murderer goes free. So what are you thinking?"

"I'm thinking I might ask Morgan to go to Peoria and talk to a few people there," Andee replied.

Bernie grabbed her chest and pretended to grapple with her heart. "Oh my gosh! You're going to ask Morgan?" She then reached her hand and pressed it to Andee's forehead. "No fever. Don't tell me you actually like the guy?"

Despite herself, Andee blushed as she pulled away from Bernie's hand and slapped at it.

"No, it's not that. He has connections down there. Besides it will give him a chance to check-up on Penny and his sister...And I have a lot of stuff to do here with the fire and all," she finished up lamely.

"You do like him," Bernie accused, laughingly. "Is it because he came through as a reliable back-up when you were rescuing those women from Parks?"

"Don't be silly. I've never liked Tubby O'Toole, and he proved to be a reliable back-up in the situation. I still don't like him."

Bernie changed tactics.

"He's really handsome, don't you think?" She rolled her eyes toward the ceiling.

"Who? Tubby?"

Bernie sputtered. "No, you idiot," she slapped

her hand over her mouth and grimaced. "I didn't mean that."

Andee was laughing.

"I meant Morgan, silly. I've had a crush on him since I first met him and he treats me like his little sister. You don't suppose he is afraid of my brothers, do you?"

As she rambled, Andee recovered herself enough to add to her musings.

"Are you kidding? Everyone is afraid of your brothers. You can say what you want about not finding Mr. Right, but even if he showed up, your brothers would give him second thoughts."

"But not if Mama liked him," Bernie laughed. "If Mama liked him, the boys would lay low."

"So, doesn't your mom like Morgan?" Andee asked mischievously.

"Of course she does… Oh you!! You're turning this around to be about me! Tell me the truth. You do like Morgan, don't you?"

Andee grinned and held up her thumb and forefinger about a half inch apart. "About this much," she said. "He's sort of growing on me." And then she blushed despite her efforts not to.

Bernie wisely dropped the subject.

Together they cleaned up their lunch and placed the leftovers in the refrigerator. As they walked out on the front porch, Bernie sighed. "What a view!"

Indeed, the wind had picked up again and cleared the valley of smoke. They stood there and gazed at the mountains to the west. Smoke still billowed up from the south and some of the flames from the back burning above the 261 could be seen. But the mountains held their attention.

"I can see why you wanted to build here," Bernie told her. "I can just see you sitting out here, gazing at the mountains and letting the view restore your soul. I need a haven like this."

"You're welcome to come sit, any time you want," Andee told her. "Just let me know when you're coming so I won't shoot you."

The girls laughed and headed for their vehicles.

"Do you think they delivered papers today?" Andee asked. "I think I'll stop by and pick one up if they did. My mom called this morning and news of Parks' capture has already hit the front page. She was fit to be tied."

Bernie smiled thinking of the sheriff's mom. She wasn't an easy woman to rattle, but the news of her daughter being shot, might do the trick. "You mean you didn't tell her you'd been shot?"

"No. I told my dad. Besides," she protested, "I wasn't really shot. I was wearing Kevlar. I thought if he wanted her to know, he'd tell her. Evidently he waited too long." Andee laughed. "Kicking *his* butt will take up most of her day. She won't call again unless something awful happens and she hears of it."

They parted at the end of Andee's drive way. Bernie continued down the east side of the hill on Maricopa Street to patrol the town's east side, and Andee turned left up over the hill and down to the Safeway store on the west side.

The store was empty except for one cashier and a manager. There may have been other employees in the meat department and the deli, but she purchased her paper and left without leaving the front of the store.

Back at the county complex, she entered the sheriff's office, spoke briefly to Sandra, and retreated to her office.

The Wallow Fire was still the biggest news, covering most of the front page; however on the bottom half of the page, a blurb two columns wide with an old campaign picture of her at the top, filled the space. No wonder her mother had been so upset. The headlines read *'Round Valley sheriff, Andrea Taylor, shot in attempted rescue'*. The story contained a statement from her office, thanks to Sandra. The article said that the women who had been kidnapped could not be reached for comment. *'Bet Morgan had something to do with that. She owed him.'* There were pictures of

Melba Wilson and Penny Dixon with a brief history of their 'alleged' kidnapping and rescue.

Next to that a follow-up story on the Roma Montgomery murder. A photo of Roma Montgomery and her family with a headline that read, *'Wallow Fire gives up a body in the White Mountains.'* The story line stated her body had been found and taken from the forest just moments before the fire had reached the spot where she had been dumped. The reporter speculated that her kidnapping was linked with the other two, but details were skimpy *'as the sheriff's office had no comments on this ongoing investigation.'* The rest was about her family and memorial service information.

Chapter 21
Sunday, June 12, 2013
A Bit More
Than She's Letting On

John Wilson joined his crew at the Sawmill Restaurant. He accepted their teasing easily. Ever since the harrowing trip to the Big Lake tower and rousting Amy Holland out and down the mountain they had suspected there was something more than friendship going on between their captain and the fire lookout lady. He had been antsy for the four days between that incident and Tuesday when their mandatory five days off came up. They'd teased him then about getting to town to Amy, but when he'd disappeared off the radar for five days, they suspected he'd spent them with that pretty young woman from the tower.

"So are we going to hear wedding bells any time

soon?" Wendy Thompson asked him.

Steve Connors scoffed. "Wedding bells? You girls are all alike. Can't wait to trap a man into marriage. Just because a guy gets sweet on a girl, doesn't mean he has to marry her, right John?"

John shrugged. "I dunno, Steve. Marriage isn't such a bad thing. My mom and dad have been married a long time. My dad adores my mom. Says he'll live a lot longer with her to take care of him."

"Yeah, but marriage is different today than it was when your folks got married. People expected you to get married and live happily ever after. Times have changed. No one gets married any more. Too complicated."

John shook his head. "That's where you're wrong, buddy-boy." He grinned at his partners. "I'm thinking that I'd be a fool to pass this one up, and if I don't marry her, some other sap is going to come along and sweep her off her feet." He turned to Wendy. "I think you might be hearing wedding bells."

Gwen whooped and slapped him on the back. "Congratulations! When?"

John looked sheepish. "Well, congratulations aren't in order quite yet. I haven't asked her, so don't be broadcasting it about."

"You haven't asked her?" Wendy exclaimed. "What kind of idiot are you? You tell us you're going to marry her, but you haven't even asked her yet? Does she know how you feel about her?"

"Well, yes. I told her that. We just never got around to talking about, well, we talked about it, I just never popped the question."

This time all of them whooped with laughter.

"John, John, John," Wendy sighed. "You're hopeless."

The waitress came and brought them more coffee and took their breakfast order. While they waited for their food, they shared stories and events from their days off.

The updated news of the day was that the residents of Round Valley would be allowed to return home before nightfall. There was no progress on containment of the fire, but it looked like the threat to the town was over. Smoke still hung heavy in the air. Residents with breathing or heart problems were advised not to return until the air cleared up.

The fire had burned across the Arizona-New Mexico border northeast of Alpine. The Big Lake fire lookout tower was not the only fire tower to be destroyed in the fire. Escudilla lookout tower, in the Escudilla Wilderness area on top of Escudilla Mountain also had been burned within the same time period of the Big Lake tower.

"So, how is Amy taking it?" Wendy asked John.

John shook his head, remembering the nights he had held her as she'd cried over the loss. "Not well. It's more than just the loss of her job. The lookout tower was built in 1933. It was one of the few wooden structures left. That tower had seen all the changes in forest management over the years. She had visited with so many of the former lookouts and gathered information. She has notes from every conversation. I think it would have been a lot worse for her if she hadn't managed to save her notes. She always carried a notebook with her and wrote down things people told her. I think she might write a book about its history."

"Do you think they'll rebuild it?"

He shrugged. "Amy thinks they won't. She can argue all the reasons why they should, but with funding cuts, she thinks it's not likely."

"What about Escudilla?"

"Probably. Who knows?"

They finished their breakfast and loaded into John's crew cab truck waiting in the parking lot. He drove them out of the parking lot and to the Forest Service Yard where they loaded into their engine truck. Leave time was over. A monster fire beckoned.

They arrived at the command center and John got out to confer with the officials gathered there and gain the latest since the crew's absence. He left the command center and walked back to the truck. "Looks like we're splitting up for the day," he told his crew. "Steve, you'll hit the road block at the 260-261 junction and relieve one of the sheriff's deputies there. Tom, Gwen, you're in Alpine and Wendy and I will be cleaning up in Nutri. There are vehicles waiting." He pointed them out and they all parted going their separate ways.

Bernie hailed Steve Connors as he walked towards the vehicles waiting to dispense personnel to their varied locations. He walked towards her vehicle with a frown on his face, but smiled at the sight of the pretty deputy. "You my ride?" he asked.

"If you're headed to relieve a road block, then that would be me," Bernie told him. "Hop in."

They introduced themselves and Bernie pulled out onto the road towards Central Avenue. After a few minutes on the road, Steve broke the silence.

"How long have you been with the sheriff's department?"

Bernie grinned. "About a year. And it's sheriff's office, not department. Our sheriff is an elected official, thus, sheriff's office. Had she been hired it would be a department." She smiled and continued, "I was hired shortly after Sheriff Taylor was elected."

"What made you choose law enforcement?"

She shrugged. "Several things. But probably

because three of my brothers are cops. "

"How many brothers do you have?"

"Six."

He whistled. "Any sisters?"

"She grinned wickedly. "Nope. I'm the baby. Spoiled and protected."

"Is that a warning?" Steve asked her.

"Does it need to be?" she countered.

Steve was silent.

Bernie smiled inwardly. Mention of six older brothers always put a damper on any would-be suitor.

She evaluated her first impression of Steve Connors as they continued to drive west. They crossed the Little Colorado River and at the top of the hill she picked up speed.

Connors was tall. Well over six feet. He looked lean and muscular, probably from all the training that went in as a firefighter. She judged him to be about 32, maybe a bit older. He was nice looking. Not over the top like Morgan Freeman, but not bad. His best feature was clear blue eyes, and a dimple in his right cheek that doubled in depth when he smiled. A slight sprinkling of freckles covered his cheeks, and reddish-brown hair peeped out from under the Arizona Cardinals ball cap he wore. He wasn't wearing a wedding ring, but in his line of work, that didn't always mean a man wasn't married.

A quick vision of red headed children with deep dimples in both cheeks filled her head. She quickly shook it away. One of those kids looked just like him, the other like her.

With his good looks, he probably wasn't used to rethinking his approach to women. She decided to give him a break.

"How long have you worked for the forest service?"

He started. "Oh, about 12 years. I graduated from forestry school and got hired in forestry management in Montana. After a few months I realized I didn't like being cooped up in an office, so I started fire training. I stayed in Montana on a hotshot crew for a while, then went to Colorado. My folks lived in Denver. Their health started failing and they decided to try a drier climate and moved to Sierra Vista. I couldn't take the heat, but it's only a four to five hour drive down there, so I put in for a position here about four years ago."

"So I guess you like the work?"

"Yeah. The money is fairly good. I like working in the woods. With flex time I usually have a three day weekend. That gives me time to go see my folks every two weeks. The other weekends I work around my place." He grinned sheepishly. "I usually have a pretty big garden every year. Looks like this year a garden will be somewhat of a challenge."

Bernie nodded her agreement. They were silent the rest of the way. They pulled up to the junction and parked. A deputy sauntered towards the Tahoe as they disembarked.

"Hey, Bernie." He greeted her and shook hands with Steve when they were introduced. "I think Steve here was supposed to relieve me, but my partner is sicker than a dog. I was just going to put a call in when I heard you were coming out. Can you get someone else out here to relieve us both?"

Bernie lifted her cell phone and punched in the sheriff's number. After explaining the situation, she told Andee she'd stay until someone else was free to relieve her. They bid the two deputies goodbye and settled in to road block duty.

Several residents dotted the foothills at the beginning of SR261. The road actually was closed to the public seven miles further up. At that point a gate, which was usually used only in the winter months to close the road, could be swung across the highway and locked. Road blocks were set up at the junction to warn non-residents that the road to Crescent Lake and Big Lake was closed and save them from having to turn back when they reached the locked gate.

Bernie wondered why anyone would want to venture into the path of such a monster fire, but admitted that some people were just idiots and death was the only cure for their stupidity. Hopefully, the road blocks would prevent that cure.

The two settled in. Traffic was meager. Residents were being allowed back into Round Valley, but most had chosen Highway 60 to return to their homes.

They talked. Bernie found the man a bit cocky. He flirted with her big time as he talked. She learned that Steve was an only child. "I was a big surprise," he told her. "Best thing that ever happened to my mom," he grinned.

His mother was 49 when he was born. His father had worked small sawmills as a millwright and saw-yer until the 1980's when big industry had pushed the smaller business out. His parents were in their early 80's and in good health considering their age. Since he was a late-in-life-baby, they determined they would teach him the importance of hard work, earning one's way and being independent.

"So they broke all the child labor laws when you were a child?"

"Oh yeah, I was so mistreated. They made me do the dishes, clean my room, weed the garden, mow the lawn and dig ditches. If I wanted a bike, I had to earn it. I paid cash for my first car after mowing lawns and doing odd jobs for three years. It was an old clunker, but it ran and I thought it was perfect."

"They must be proud of you now."

Steve laughed and ducked his head. "I don't think they planned to live this long."

Bernie wasn't sure how to take most of his flamboyant statements. To say he was over confident and egotistical was her first impression. However; as the day progressed she caught glimpses of insecurities and wondered if some of that ego didn't stem from that.

"You aren't married?" Steve asked her.

"Nope."

Bernie told him about her two tours of the Middle East while in the National Guard and her determination to make law enforcement a career. She laughed when she described each of her older brothers and watched his face as he digested the information.

He laughed when she told him what a disappointment she was to her mother who wanted her to marry and give her grandchildren.

"So aren't any of your brothers married? Don't they have kids?"

"Oh, sure. They're all married except Sam and Joe. Jake, the oldest has three kids. Alan has four. Jared has four, and David is just older than me. He has one and a baby on the way. But Mama says it's just not the same. 'Meja,' she says to me. 'Wait unteel you have daughters, O Dios, if you ever do, then you weel *know.'* " Bernie mimicked her mom's Mexican accent.

"So your mom is Mexican. Not your dad though? Fite? Where does that name come from?"

"Mom's from Sonora. She came to the U.S. as a baby. Her parents had great sponsors and they became citizens right away. My grandmother had a hard time learning English, so my mom is bilingual and still takes on a Mexican accent when she is upset or worried. My dad's folks are second generation Swiss, thus the name Fite."

It was well after three o'clock in the afternoon before anyone came to relieve Bernie. Steve would probably remain on road block duty another four hours. Bernie shook his hand and grinned at him. "You know for a spoiled brat and an only child, I really enjoyed talking to you. Maybe I'll see you around after they get this thing under control."

Bernie drove away without a backwards glance, but she suddenly felt as if she was leaving something important behind. She shook away the feeling and headed for the sheriff's office.

———— ◆((◦))◆ ————

Andee sighed and leaned back into her chair. She stretched her arms above her head, winced as the bruise on her chest reminded her it was still there, and yawned. Wednesday night the monster fire had ripped through the village of Greer, just fifteen miles west of Round Valley. Andee was up most of the night, listening to reports from her officers and the firefighters at the blaze. Her heart pounded as she listened to the radio. The efforts to save the town had been touch and go for a while.

There were two parts of Greer. Snuggled against the canyon wall, east of the Little Colorado River, 30 or 40 homes lined the county road that dead-ended about three miles inward. The western side and the main part of the village, housed the few small businesses, lodges and resorts. State Route 373 ended at the top of the hill before entering Greer, thus it was known as "The Road to Nowhere." County road 1120 carried traffic through the village where it ended a couple of miles up the canyon.

The canyon had acted like a chimney when the fire struck the little town, sucking the flame from the south end to the north end so quickly that firefighters had feared for their lives and those of the few stubborn residents who refused to leave.

One firefighter had told the reporter for a Phoenix television station that the smoke had become so thick that visibility was impossible.

Thank God, no lives were lost in those harried

moments when man and beast fought for the upper hand. So far twenty homes on the eastern canyon slope had been reported destroyed.

Andee had been busy all morning making phone calls to homeowners and fielding calls from concerned residents.

Her dad had called. They had not returned when the evacuation had lifted. He told her that her mother was having a good time visiting with her Aunt Jean and they were going to wait until the air quality cleared up some more before coming home. Meanwhile, would Andee go check the house and clear out the refrigerator in case anything had been left that would ruin?

Andee grinned to herself. As if her mother would leave anything in the refrigerator that might ruin. She'd already plied her with the contents of the fridge when they had evacuated. Andee had been eating on it all week. Still, she would check the house and water her mother's flowers, to keep her happy.

She stretched again, and rose from her desk. Might as well take care of that little task while she was awake, because another hour at her desk and she'd just put her head down and sleep.

She informed Sandra of her intentions and left the office.

She met Bernie in the parking lot.

"Thought you might want to get some supper at the Mill," Bernie told her. "I'm famished."

"Sure. I just have to run by my folks' place and check a few things. I'll meet you there in half an hour, if you can wait that long."

Bernie laughed. "I can't, but I'll order an appetizer until you get there."

Half an hour later Andee joined Bernie at their favorite table near the kitchen. Business was slow and Jason was standing at the table laughing with Bernie. When Andee appeared, he saluted her with two fingers and moved so she could take a chair.

"I'm really glad to see you Sheriff," he said. "I can't believe Sheriff Parks would let his men try and burn you alive." He shuddered. "That's just mean, nasty, and wrong!"

Andee thanked him for his concern and ordered a hamburger with fries. When he left their table, she turned her attention to Bernie.

"So how's road block duty?"

Bernie grinned. "Not bad, actually."

"Really? Since when?" Everyone complained about road block duty; especially when everyone wanted to be in on the action... on the front lines. Road block was especially boring, and hot.

Bernie shrugged. "Time really passed fast today. I partnered with a firefighter and we had a lot to talk about."

"Uh huh," Andee prompted. "And…?"

"Nothing." Bernie blushed. "We just hit it off. That's all. He's kind of egotistical, but nice underneath."

Andee was skeptical, but she let the matter drop. When Bernie was ready, she would talk about it. But Andee suspected there was more than she was letting on.

Chapter 22
"I'm Sure The Police
Did Their Job, Sheriff"

By June 15, the power had been restored to the towns of Alpine and Nutrioso. Authorities reported a ten percent containment of the fire on Sunday and eighteen percent at the end of the day on Tuesday. Winds had died a bit, but they were expected to pick up over the weekend. It was important that as much as possible be done for containment before the winds picked up again.

The fire had torched over 469,407 acres, making the Wallow Fire the largest wild fire in Arizona history, displacing the Rodeo-Chedeski Fire in 2002, that burned 467,000 acres. That fire had come very close to the towns of Show Low and Pinetop-Lakeside and smoke from its blaze had settled in Round Valley for several days.

Hilton Parks had been arraigned and charged with five counts of kidnapping, four counts of attempted murder, attempted arson, and identity theft. He was being held in the Apache County Jail Complex without bond. His flunkies faced the same charges. His son, Connie, whom Andee suspected was an accomplice, had been detained at the Canadian border with a false passport and I.D. He faced federal charges for trying to leave the country with false papers. He also would be transported back to Apache County when the feds were finished with him to stand trial with his father on the kidnapping and identity theft charges. He'd dodged the bullet by not being at the Blanton place and would not have attempted murder tacked onto his list of crimes.

Morgan had called from Phoenix. He had little more information than they had already gleaned on the Montgomery case. Roma's boss told him that she and her husband had fought a lot and that she came to work often wearing sunglasses and long sleeved blouses. Some of the bruises could not be concealed. Frank Rosencrans, the owner of the Rosencrans Funeral and Cremations said she was a good employee, but always insisted on leaving at precisely five p.m. when the business closed. She said her husband worried if she wasn't home on time. He said she had requested Friday off so she and her husband could work some things out.

"Rosencrans said he had encouraged her to get professional help, but she would clam up if he mentioned it. I drove by Roger Montgomery's house. There's a For Sale sign in the yard."

"They could have been trying to sell already," Andee told him. "A lot of people are losing their homes in this economy."

"Yeah, I know. But I'm going to check it out with the realtor before I head home. Is everything going okay there?"

"Mostly. Power was restored to Alpine and Nutri yesterday. Residents will probably be able to go home this weekend. Round Valley is almost back to normal."

"Smoke still bad?"

"Off and on. Depends on the wind."

They hung up. Andee pulled the murder file on Roma Montgomery to her and opened it up. She jotted the date on a yellow sticky note and added notes about her conversation with Morgan. As much as she wanted to pin Roma's murder on Hilton Parks and have the whole thing tied up in one nasty bundle, things just didn't fit.

Her money was on the husband, Roger Montgomery. Maybe Morgan could shed some light on that when she talked to him again. The husband?

Despite his belligerence he had seemed genuinely grieved when he'd come to identify his wife's body. Still, something just didn't feel right. But if he had killed her, how did her body get to the White Mountains? Morgan had questioned his boss. According to him, Roger hadn't missed any work, but he worked a four day week. His mother said Roma was taking the kids to her mother's in Apache Junction for the weekend. She talked to Roger on Saturday afternoon and assumed he was home as he said he was going to mow the lawn as soon as it cooled down a bit. He didn't file a missing person's report until Sunday night when she didn't return home with the children. But according to the police, Roma's mother was not expecting her to come for the weekend. She'd gathered up the kids herself and Roma had told her she and Roger were going to try and work a few things out.

She called Morgan's cell.

"Miss me?" he answered with a chuckle.

She got right down to business. "Have you talked to Mr. Rosencrans personally? What's your gut feeling on him?"

"Not your typical funeral director. Good looking. Rather debonair for a funeral director. If I were type casting, I'd put him in a dance studio rather than a mortuary. He's married. No kids."

"So, would he be a suspect in Roma's

disappearance?"

"His alibi in Vegas checked out. He was a keynote speaker at a funeral convention. About 600 people can vouch for him on Saturday," Morgan continued. "Where are you going with this, Andee? You don't think Parks is guilty of her kidnapping and murder?"

"It's just a feeling," she told him. "You know… that gut thing you told me about.

"Do you think you could nose around a bit? According to what you told me, Roger's mom said he stayed home all day the day Roma disappeared. Roger said she'd gone to her mother's. So according to her, Roger was home all day. But did his mother see him? Did she talk to him? Did she go over there? Did she call his home phone? Did he call her from his home phone or did he just use his cell? Do you know if the police searched his car?"

"Whoa! Slow down. I'm sure the police did their job, Sheriff."

"I'm not saying they didn't, Morgan. But in light of this 'gut feeling' I have, I just want to know exactly what they did and how far they went in the investigation. Did they stop investigating after we arrested Hilton Parks?"

"Okay. I've got a buddy or two in the Peoria PD. I'll see what I can find out. Maybe I'll drop by on Mrs. Montgomery as well."

"Thanks. I owe you one."

He chuckled. "You owe me more than one. I'll collect when things settle down." With that he broke their connection.

Andee smiled. She was pretty sure Morgan had been flirting with her. She wasn't too experienced in that area, but... How did she feel about that? She had to admit, it didn't bother her as much as she thought it would. He had proven to be totally different from the P.I.s she'd judged him by, mainly one Ramsey Ratliff. She was pretty sure Ratliff had crawled out from under a fresh cow pie.

Morgan, on the other hand, was liked by most everyone who knew him. He seemed honest, caring. His niece Penny thought the world of him. His brother-in-law, Don, seemed to have a lot of respect for him. Andee smiled to herself. She was pretty sure her mom and dad would like him, too.

She'd been staring at the Montgomery murder file for fifteen minutes without making a single notation worthy of investigation. There were however flourishes and doodles in the margins of the page that she had made while her mind wandered over the character of one Private Investigator, Morgan Freeman.

She shoved the pages back into the file and locked them up. This was silly. She'd known him for less than two weeks. This was not like the Andee Taylor she knew. The cautious Andee Taylor. The no-nonsense about men Andee Taylor. Nope, nope, nope. This was not like her at all.

━━━━━━●(●)●━━━━━━

Morgan pressed the end button on his smart phone, but held the phone a few seconds, just staring at it, as if he could conjure up an image to go with the voice he had just hung up on.

He hadn't been interested in a woman, any woman, since Gyllian. He was surprised that the memory of her didn't take him back into the black void this time. When had he climbed out of that dark tunnel of grief? He delved back into the recent weeks and realized he had not even thought of her for a while. He shrugged off the small niggle of guilt that threatened. It had been five years. New Year's Eve was probably the last time he'd felt the loneliness. Would he have even felt it then if he'd not allowed his well meaning friends to drag him to a party where it was mainly couples? Probably not, he admitted.

Andee Taylor was nothing like Gyllian Moore. Gyl had been petite, blonde and blue eyed. She could look helpless at any given time, but that look was a ruse. She was as feisty and independent as any young woman ever hoped to be. She'd kept him on his toes. She had no qualms about challenging him if she disagreed with him. She always did it with such grace and tact that before the discussion was over he found himself agreeing with her. He grinned. As a matter of fact, that was why when he applied for his last drivers license he had registered to vote as a Republican instead of a Democrat. Gyl was very persuasive.

He pulled out his wallet and opened the photo section to a well worn photograph of his former fiancé. She really hadn't been all that pretty on the outside. She had a square face. Her nose was long and straight and her mouth too wide. But when she smiled her whole face lit up the room. That was what had attracted him to her in the first place. There was nothing fake about Gyllian Moore's smile. The first time she had turned its full force on him he was a goner. On the inside, the part that mattered, Gyllian had been the most beautiful woman he'd ever met.

He put the picture away, as well as the memories, and went to the kitchen to find his sister.

Chapter 23
Is It A Lucrative Business?

By mid-week, twenty-three days after the Wallow Fire started, officials said containment was fifty-eight percent. An end was finally in sight. The winds had settled a bit, but it was still hot and dry. The possibility of rain had been predicted for the weekend. New burn areas spread slower, therefore the damage was smaller. In New Mexico, the small village of Luna and the community of Escudilla Bonita Acres on the north eastern side of Escudilla Mountain were still on stand-by for evacuation, but it was looking better all the time. Reserve, the county seat of Catron County, New Mexico had taken on the look of a bustling city with over a thousand fire-fighters and National Guard situated there to help protect the lives and abodes of those settlements.

Residents of Alpine and Nutrioso had been allowed to return to their homes on Saturday, the eighteenth. Greer residents had returned the following Tuesday.

Those who lived in the Blue area, south of Alpine, were still waiting for the all clear.

Andee's parents were home. Anita had called her as they entered town. "Oh, what a wonderful way to welcome us home," she declared when Andee answered her phone.

"How's that, Mom?" she asked.

"The little digital sign on the trailer at the edge of town that says, '*Welcome Home*', she said. "What a nice homey touch."

Andee smiled. "Oh, I did that just for you, Mom. The moment I knew you were coming home I had the guys take that trailer out there."

"Sure you did sweetheart. It's a nice touch, though. I'm sure there were a lot of people who didn't know if they would have a home or not when they got back. So those little signs are nice."

"Are you coming to supper tonight? Your dad and I would really like to see you. If you're not too busy that is."

Andee agreed, but only if her mother was sure she was up to it.

Her mother laughed. "Of course I'm up to it. Be here at five so we'll have time to visit before supper."

Cooking was her mother's passion and if she

could cook for guests, even her own daughter, she would get off her deathbed to cook a meal.

Her phone rang again before she could lay it down. She smiled.

"Good afternoon. This is Sheriff Taylor."

"Well, hello Sheriff Taylor. This is your friendly, despicable Private Eye, Morgan Freeman. Got a minute?"

"Sure," Andee informed him, "but wait! Who said you were despicable?"

Morgan laughed. "Well, no one actually said it, but I did get a certain impression when we met..." He paused. "Listen, I just got back. I might have something. Do you want to go have some dinner somewhere? I'm starved."

Andee told him she was already committed to her mother for dinner, but he was welcome to tag along. After a little cajoling, she convinced him he would be welcome and he agreed. She quickly called her mother to tell her to set an extra place.

"Morgan Freeman," she mused. "Isn't that the man who was with you when you Hilton Parks shot you? The one who shot Hilton? Juanita was telling me about him. She says he's a very nice man."

Andee laughed. "Mom, the entire Fite family adores Morgan Freeman. They are convinced if God died, Morgan could take His place."

"Andrea Rebecca Taylor!" her mother exclaimed.

"I was just joking, mom." Andrea blushed. She knew the minute the words flew from her mouth her mother would take exception to them. Even in jest.

"Well, you just show some respect, do you hear? I will not have a daughter of mine disrespecting the Lord God Almighty."

"I know, Mom, I'm sorry. It's okay if I bring Morgan along?"

She glanced at her watch. Only 4:30. She punched in Morgan's number on her cell phone and waited for him to answer. She told him how to get to her parent's house and told him she would meet him there at five.

She hadn't meant to change clothes, but, she told herself, she'd been wearing this uniform since yesterday. There was time for a quick shower and a change if she hurried. She was already shoving the Tahoe in gear and roaring up the road towards her own little house on the hill.

She wasted a bit of time debating on a pair of jeans and a shirt, or a simple skirt and blouse. Who was she kidding? If she wore the skirt and blouse, her dad was bound to say something about it, since the only time she wore a dress of any kind was to church, weddings, parties and funerals. Then Morgan would know she'd worn it to impress him.

Well, she wasn't trying to impress him, she told herself. She was the sheriff, after all. She needed to be practical. If he wanted impressed, well he could just bark up another tree.

She did choose a pink blouse, knowing she looked good in it. She combed her hair, then tousled it with her fingers and left the house.

She met Morgan on the corner. He was waiting, parked on the side of the road and motioned to her that he would follow her rest of the way.

Andee allowed herself to be swallowed in a gigantic hug from her mother. She laughed. "Geeze, Mom, one would think you had been gone for a year. It's only been a couple of weeks."

Anita pushed her away and laughed, wiping tears from her eyes.

"Honey, you were shot! You could have been killed! Give your mother a break."

Andee introduced Morgan to her parents. Her dad immediately took him out into the back yard for a chat, while Andee helped her mom finish up their supper. Andee knew Morgan was telling her dad of the events at the Blanton place, so she touched lightly on how she and Morgan came to be there together and the events leading up to the capture of Parks and his men. Her mother listened quietly, which surprised Andee, since as a school teacher, she was usually very inquisitive, asking questions at every break in the conversation. When Andee told her about Penny capturing the rattlesnake and threatening to throw it into the midst of the former sheriff's men, Anita's face blanched. She griped the counter and her knuckles turned white.

"Mom, are you okay?" Andee rounded the counter and put her arm around her mom's shoulders.

Anita smiled wanly. "I'm fine, Hon. I was just thinking about that young woman taking such a chance. I don't think I could do something like that. What was she thinking?"

Ben Taylor's large form filled the back door as he entered from the yard. He swooped in with an exaggerated hug and a kiss for his wife. "I'm thinking she was thinking that desperate means demand desperate measures. That little girl saved the day, and our little girl, Mama. When's supper?" And as quickly as that, he changed the subject and began helping the women carry food to the table waiting on the back porch.

As promised, Anita hadn't gone to a lot of trouble. There was a big summer salad with fruit and vegetables and a raspberry dressing, fresh cauliflower and broccoli steamed to perfection and chicken breasts marinated in buttermilk and garlic and grilled. Large glasses of raspberry iced tea set at each place. On the side table a strawberry rhubarb pie cooled. Andee knew her mother probably had fresh, frozen pies in the freezer, so all she had to do was bring one out and put it in the oven.

"So, Mr. Freeman, Andee tells me you're a private investigator?"

Morgan wiped his mouth and swallowed his food before answering her.

"Yes, ma'am. And it's Morgan, please. I always have a tendency to look around for my dad when I hear Mr. Morgan."

Morgan told her about his years as a cop in the valley, and how the politics had gotten the best of his better attitude, so he'd decided to pack it in rather than apply to a smaller department where the politics might be worse. He told her he had been a good investigative officer with Chandler PD and later with Maricopa County, so it just fell into place that he would or should do what he did best.

"But do you have enough work up here for it to be a lucrative business?" Anita asked.

"No," Morgan laughed. "Good question, Anita. Most of my clients come out of the Phoenix area. I do a lot of traveling. I have a small apartment in Chandler, but I spend a lot of time at my sister's. I'm not here, at home, as often as I would like to be, but I have a good secretary for when I'm out of the office and a good hired hand for when I'm not at the ranch. It's not often that a case from there brings me to the mountains, but when it does, I am not going to look a gift horse in the mouth."

"And neither are we," Ben told him. "We will never be able to thank you enough for being there with Andee at the Blanton place."

"Don't forget, my niece was the main reason I was there," Morgan shrugged off the gratitude and praise as if it was the most common thing in the world for him to be there.

Andee allowed her mom and dad to command the conversation with Morgan. She learned a lot about the man as she listened. To her dismay, he learned a lot about her, as her parents were more than willing to volunteer tidbits about her growing up years.

"And you're not married?" Anita asked innocently. Andee choked on her raspberry iced tea. Grabbing a napkin, she covered her mouth as she coughed and sputtered. When she'd finally gotten her choking under control, she made a face at her mom.

Morgan and Ben laughed.

"I'm not married." By this time he was calling her parents by their first names. "I was engaged. My fiancé died."

"I'm sorry." Anita's eyes focused on his face as if searching for more than he was giving in the simple statement.

"I have good memories," Morgan told her.

As if the answer was what she was seeking, Anita started to clear the table. "Why don't you men stay out here on the porch while Andee and I clean up. Would you like some coffee?"

Twenty minutes later the kitchen was spotless and they were all sitting on the back porch sipping coffee and talking. The conversation moved from the Wallow Fire, to what it was like before the fire and what they hoped would happen after the fire.

Officials were predicting, as in previous wildfires that with all the vegetation gone from the forests there would be nothing to hold the water once the rains started. Flooding would likely follow the containment of the fire. It would be years before the forests could be proclaimed healthy again.

As far as the town, they'd had a great idea bringing tourists in with rodeos and craft bazaars throughout the summer months. Ben said he hoped they would not let this year's fire squelch those plans and they would continue with the summer fun the next year.

It was after eight when Andee and Morgan said their goodbyes and left the Taylor's house. As they walked to their cars, Morgan asked if she still wanted to hear what he'd uncovered while in the valley or if she wanted to wait until morning and go over it in the office.

"Well, now that you mention it, I doubt I'll be able to sleep from wondering, so why don't we go over the high points tonight and sleep on the over-all," she said to him. She started to climb into her Tahoe when it dawned on her that they hadn't discussed where they would go. She hesitated. She was pretty sure they were both coffee-d out, and she'd spent most of her day at the office and didn't really want to go back.

Before she could change her mind, she asked, "Do you want to follow me to my place? I don't think I could swallow another sip of coffee and I've been in the office all day. I'd just like to take my shoes off and relax."

"Why, Sheriff Andee. I do believe I've moved up a notch in your book if you're actually inviting me into your home."

Andee gave him a shove and started her engine, letting him follow if he wanted. He did.

Chapter 25
Sugar Wouldn't
Melt In His Mouth

Andee unlocked the door and entered her little house. Flipping on the light, she was suddenly relieved that in her rush to shower and change clothes earlier in the evening she had taken everything to the bedroom. Her little part of the world was neat and tidy.

She expected Morgan to follow her in, but when she turned he was still standing at the door, facing the western horizon. The sun had set and the clouds covered the western sky. They glowed with orange and purple and all shades in between. She stepped up behind him.

"Wow," he said.

"Breathtaking, isn't it? It's not just the sunsets, you know? From up here the scene changes daily, sometimes hourly. It's never the same."

He turned and smiled at her, moving into the house. "So how long have you lived here?"

"In this house? About five years. I had some money from my grandmother, so when I got out of college, I decided to build. When I was a teenager, I used to ride my bike up here when I needed to be alone." She giggled. "I thought I had the cares of the world on my shoulders."

She moved to the refrigerator. "Do you want something to drink? I've got tea? Soda? Water?"

Morgan asked for water and she chose one for herself as well.

"Shall we sit at the counter?"

They pulled up stools and sat side by side, shoulders almost touching. Morgan opened his tooled briefcase and pulled out a file.

"Okay," he said. "Roma Montgomery. Something is rotten in Denmark. Like you, I'm pretty sure Hilton Parks is not guilty of this murder. And I like the husband for it more and more. Proving it? I think we have our work cut out for us."

He had made an appointment with the realtor as a potential buyer to look at the Montgomery house. "I told her I'd been looking in that neighborhood and couldn't find anything. She volunteered that the listing was new. It was listed only two days after Roma's memorial service."

"That's not much to go on," Andee said. "People sell their houses after their spouses die. They lose that second income and find they can't afford the payments."

Morgan nodded.

He'd talked to Roma's mother, Mrs. Alba. According to her, the marriage had been rocky for a few years. Roger had been mentally abusive almost from the start, but after Roma got pregnant with the third child, he started hitting her. She said he was always sorry and would beg for forgiveness, but it happened over and over again. Lately, Roma had been talking about leaving him, but she was afraid. Mrs. Alba said she was pretty sure that is why she sent the kids to her for the weekend. She figured if she could get away without having to worry about the safety of the children she would be able to file for divorce once she was settled somewhere.

"So why didn't she go to her mother's house?"

"Fear. Roger threatened to kill her and anyone who helped her if she left him. She didn't want to put her mother or the kids in jeopardy."

"Nice guy," Andee said.

"Well, yes," Morgan drawled. "According to *his* mother, sugar wouldn't melt in his mouth. He doted on Roma and his children. He was a good husband.

But Roma just wouldn't let him have a life outside of the family. She insisted on going to work when the youngest started school so they could buy that big ole house."

Andee waited. "Detective Raymond checked his financials. They bought the house shortly after getting married, so that shoots holes in his mother's story. Five years ago, they were slowly going under. He'd run up some major credit card debt at the casinos. About $100,000. It looks like Roma started working to help get them out of debt. Two months after she started working at Rosencrans Funeral all their credit cards were canceled and there were no more credit card charges. Both their checks were direct deposit. Payments were made monthly to pay off the credit cards. They still owe about $75,000 on their home. He has it listed for $225,000."

Morgan sketched a detailed account of his investigation. Unfortunately, there was not enough evidence against Roger to get a search warrant. However, he had agreed to let the police search his car without a warrant. They found nothing out of the ordinary. No blood in or out of the car. Just the normal prints from all the family members and a couple of unidentified, but they were children's prints, so the police surmised they were probably friends of the Montgomery's children who had ridden in the car at one time or another.

At Roma's mother's suggestion, Morgan had talked to Roma's best friend since high school, Selma Wright. She said that maybe Roma would share things with her friend that she was reluctant to share with her mother.

Selma said that yes, Roma was planning to leave Roger. And she was planning to file for a divorce as soon as she got settled. She was going to leave the kids with her mother and file for custody when she got the divorce, but she didn't want to take them with her out of state, because she knew Roger would put up a fuss and try and take them from her. Selma also told him that she thought something else was going on with Roma. That she'd seemed worried and somewhat secretive.

Selma told him that Roger wasn't a drinker. He was just plain mean. He was mentally and physically abusive. One time he had beaten Roma so badly that she had been in the hospital for two weeks recovering. Roma told the doctors she had been mugged and she signed into the hospital under an assumed name. She'd checked herself out without paying the bill, but had purchased a money order every payday to pay off the hospital bill.

"Selma said she was like that," Morgan said. "She hated owing people and even if she skipped out on a bill, she would pay a bit every payday until it was paid."

Morgan also had talked to Roma's oldest child, a fourteen year old boy who stopped him at the gas pump at the market just down the street from his grandmother's. He had wanted to know if Morgan had figured out who had killed his mother.

"I got the feeling he suspected his father," Morgan said, shaking his head.

The boy said his mother and father fought most of the time, so he and his siblings were always glad to go to his grandmothers for the weekend. He said his father was really a jerk, but not like with his mom, although it seemed that the older he got the tougher his dad was on him.

"So there was nothing in the car to indicate foul play or that Roma had been in it under adverse circumstances?" Andee asked, biting her lower lip. "Did they check to see if he'd rented a car someplace?"

"Actually, they checked out the three places closest to where he lives, but there was no record of any Roger Montgomery renting a car. Detective Raymond said she would extend the search to rental places near the mortuary, but didn't hold much hope."

"So, we both feel the husband is good for the murder, but there is no evidence to support our suspicions. His alibi doesn't hold water, but not having an alibi isn't enough for a search warrant. Roma was going to leave and get a divorce. Her mother thought that was the plan for the weekend, so she didn't check to see if Roma was home. I thought she said she was taking off so she could work things out with Roger."

"That was her initial story until she realized that her son-in-law may have murdered her daughter." He grinned. "She's been more open and forthcoming since then. I think she thinks he's good for it too."

"Basically, we're back at square one, then. Great."

"Detective Raymond is still on the case and I get the feeling she's pretty tenacious. She has promised to keep us in the loop."

Andee swung around and stepped down off her stool. Stretching, she padded to the refrigerator and extracted a water.

"How's Penny?"

Morgan grinned. "How do you think? She's already back to work at the funeral home."

Andee laughed. "That sounds like her. I wouldn't put anything past a girl who would wrangle a rattlesnake to stop the bad guys. She's the spunkiest teenager I've ever met. Did you see Melba while you were down there?"

"I did. She's enjoying her new grandbaby. I think she and her husband agree that it's time she stayed home and enjoyed her grandkids. She's talking about becoming a full time babysitter once the trial is over. She's already preparing for her testimony."

Andee motioned for Morgan to follow her into the living room and indicated he should sit on the couch. She perched on the glider rocker opposite him.

They were silent for a few moments. It was a comfortable silence. Andee marveled. She could not remember a time when she'd been in the same room with a man when in the silence she wasn't trying to figure out something to say.

"I apologize, Morgan."

He looked at her with a puzzled frown. "For what?"

"You know, for acting so uppity when I first met you. I'm not usually like that. There's no excuse for my behavior, and I'm sorry."

Morgan chuckled. "I hadn't noticed."

"Right." Andee laughed. Morgan joined her. It seemed once they started they couldn't stop and every time they looked at each other the laughter would begin again. She wiped tears from her eyes and snatched a tissue from the box on the end table.

When they were finally in control, Andee re-marked, "You know, if either of us told someone else why we were laughing we wouldn't be able to explain. It's one of those *you had to be there* things.

"Kind of a mental and physical let down from all the stress over the past three or four weeks," he agreed. "I don't think I've laughed that hard since Gyl was alive."

He was silent for a few moments.

"Can I tell you about her?"

His sister had introduced them. They were co-workers. They'd hit it off right from the start. He fell in love with her the first time he saw her, but it wasn't until he hadn't seen her for three days afterwards that he realized just how hard he had fallen. After that they were inseparable. They had dated only three months when he proposed. She was finishing her degree in Elementary Education and they'd agreed to wait to get married until she was out of school.

"We just wanted something simple. A few friends. Our families. We put a down payment on a little house in a good neighborhood in Mesa. She got a job teaching first grade, not far from there."

Andee waited, watching his face change as the memories flooded back.

They had both wanted children. They'd agreed on two boys and two girls, as if they could decide what they were actually going to have. Pets were okay, but not until the children were older and could learn responsibility and help take care of them.

He wanted a ranch. A small piece of property

in the mountains. Somewhere they could get away from the hustle and bustle of the city. He heard about the property in Vernon and decided to check it out, but Gyl had stayed behind to finish up the wedding plans. The wedding was less than a week away. She said she trusted him. He knew better than she, what he wanted. So he had driven up to the mountains. He'd liked the place and made an offer.

Gyl was excited and they made plans to eat dinner at her place and he would show her all the pictures he'd taken. She told him not to worry if she was a little late. She and her bridesmaid were in Tucson and they would be back in Mesa just shortly after he arrived back.

"She never made it home," he said. "A semi blew out a tire and lost control. He hit Gyl's car and knocked it off the highway into a car coming off the on ramp. Both cars careened off the roadway. She and her friend were killed outright."

Andee expelled the breath she hadn't realized she was holding. Her eyes were glued to Morgan's face. She could not speak. Telling him she was sorry for his loss seemed trivial and insignificant.

"I went through all the normal channels of grief," he said. "Gyl was a wonderful Christian. She wasn't just religious, you know? She lived what she believed. So when she died…" he shook his head self depreciatingly. "I was so angry. How could God let something like this happen? Gyl was always telling me that we could make all the plans we wanted, but God knew the plans he had for us, and sometimes He just laughed. All I could see for the first few months was this monster God laughing at us and all the plans we had made."

He had thrown himself into his work, volunteered for extra shifts, and literally shut down to all outside aspects of life. He quit going to church. Stopped seeing family members and drank too much.

"One night my partner and I responded to a report of teenagers breaking a window in a jewelry store. We caught sight of them about two blocks away and gave chase. They headed for an alley and Dennis bailed out of the car to follow them. I was to go around and cut them off at the end of the alley. Before I got around the block to the other end, one of them pulled a gun and shot my partner. Dennis got off two shots before he lost consciousness. I thought we'd lost him. He was in surgery for six hours and in ICU for two weeks. It was touch and go.

"His fiancé was there every day. She never lost faith. She muttered to herself all the time. I thought she was a nut and couldn't figure out what Dennis was getting himself into. It wasn't until he'd been in the hospital a week that I realized she was praying.

She prayed as she walked down the hallway to his room. She prayed at his bedside. She prayed in the waiting room. At first it drove me crazy. I wanted to yell at her that the God she was praying to just didn't care. He was going to snuff out Dennis' life just like he had my Gyllian's and all this praying she was doing was useless. But I didn't say anything. I guess I had enough sense not to add to the pain she was already suffering."

And then, one day, he had arrived at the hospital and slipped into Dennis' room. His fiancé was there alone. She didn't hear him come in. He stood silently so as not to disturb her. She was praying as usual. She wasn't pleading for Dennis' recovery. She was just talking and asking for strength and for faith so that no matter what God had planned she would go on praising Him.

"Gyl always talked to Him like He was in the same room, you know? She'd say, 'Hi Father. Did you see that big blunder I made today? I'll bet you laughed. Thank you for making me realize I'm not such a big shot.' Things like that. But I'd never heard anyone else do it.

"And then she started singing Amazing Grace. I think that is when my healing started. I just touched her on the shoulder and we held each other and cried together.

Andee sighed. "How long has it been since Gyl died?"

"Five years this month."

"And your partner, Dennis? Did he recover?"

"Mmmmhem. They got married about two weeks after he left the hospital." He chuckled. "In fact, when he got out of rehab, he turned in his resignation and went back to school. I believe he is the pastor of a little church up in Steamboat, Colorado now."

"So, are you still angry with God?" She held her breath. His answer was important to her.

"Not so much anymore. I've been hearing that still small voice in my head quite a lot lately. I kind of miss the fellowship. In fact, your dad invited me to attend church with your family this next Sunday. Would that bother you if I did?"

"Well, no…of course not. I mean, I might not go, so you know, that wouldn't bother me if I weren't there, of course, but if things settle down here in town, I might go. Mom hates it when I miss church, even if it is the job that keeps me away." She stopped. She was rambling. She blushed. "That would be great, Morgan. Whether I go or not. Mom and Dad would love to introduce you to the congregation."

Morgan rose. "I really need to go. It's almost midnight. I'm sorry. I didn't mean to keep you up so long."

"Oh no. And you still have to drive back to Vernon, then back here tomorrow. Listen, why don't you stay the night?"

Morgan raised his eyebrows.

"No," she blushed. "Not here. I mean, that didn't come out right. I meant in town. We have some comfortable cots at the office. You could sleep there tonight and you wouldn't have to drive back in tomorrow." She slipped her shoes on and grabbed her keys. "Come on. I'll show you your room."

He followed her down the hill to the sheriff's office and waited while she unlocked the door, then followed her in. She buzzed the jail area and stood in the window until the jailer came and acknowledged her. He followed her through the door to the back area.

"Hi, Clyde. Have you met Morgan Freeman?" she said in way of introductions. "We've been going over the Roma Montgomery case and time passed a little faster than we had planned. He's going to crash in one of the front cells tonight."

"Sure thing, Ma'am."

Andee led him down the hallway and showed him the men's room. "We have showers in the restrooms. There are towels and soap in the cupboard. Help yourself. There's a laundry hamper just outside the door, just deposit used towels there. The door between the front office and here is locked from six p.m. to six a.m. If you find yourself needing the facilities before six in the morning, ring the buzzer and

Clyde will let you through."

She led him back to the front offices. "The room is really deceiving. It looks like curtains are all that separate you from the main common room and office, but that's all a façade. The room is actually pretty tight. When you swing the door closed, it looks like bars across, but as you can see…" she demonstrated. Outside bars encased the door with a curtain hiding the wooden structure of the door that actually latched, making the cell a small bedroom. "You can lock it from the inside if you don't want to be disturbed."

Morgan removed his western hat and hung it on a hook inside the door.

"This is great. I'll see you in the morning, then."

She hesitated for just an instant. Morgan stepped towards her and took her chin in his hands. Leaning forward he kissed her gently on the lips. "Good night Sheriff. Thanks for a wonderful evening."

Andee touched her lips briefly, then tucked her head and turned. "Good night, Morgan."

She let herself out and checked to make sure the door was locked.

She didn't fall asleep for at least an hour after going to bed. It was just a kiss, after all. Nothing significant. So why, then did it the feel of his lips on her's linger, even an hour afterwards?

Chapter 24

You Really Didn't Think She'd Turn Me Down?

The end was in sight. Wallow Fire containment had reached eighty-two percent. Engine 62 crew members had once again gathered in the corner booth of the Sawmill Restaurant for breakfast. All, that is, except Steve Connors. He had excused himself and joined the tall, dark haired, female deputy sitting at a table near the rear of the restaurant.

Wendy raised her eyebrows and smirked. "I think our Steve is in love."

Gwen laughed and swigged her coffee. "I think our Steve had best watch his Ps and Qs if he is sweet on Bernie Fite. That is one tough deputy. She can spot a phony a mile away. Why do you think she's almost thirty and never been married?"

"Brothers?" Wendy grinned.

"Well, yeah, but if she wanted something, her brothers wouldn't stand in her way."

"John," Gwen grinned impishly. "How's your love life? Did you get around to asking Amy to marry you?"

John ducked his head. "Yep. As a matter of fact I did."

"And?" Gwen and Wendy both chimed.

"And?" John answered, a blank expression on his face.

"And… what did she say?"

John's expression instantly turned to dreamy. "Say? What did she say? Well, she said 'yes' of course! You didn't really think she'd turn me down?"

They laughed. "Maybe, if she knew what we know… stinky feet, bad breath, bad language, you know all your bad qualities."

"Me? Bad qualities?" John protested. He placed his hands over his heart. "I'm hurt. I thought we were friends."

Their breakfast came and they devoted the next few minutes digging in to hot steaming plates of green chili covered hash browns, huevos rancheros, and biscuits and gravy. When Jason had cleared their plates and refilled their coffee mugs, the talk turned to current events in the town. They exhausted the latest on the Wallow Fire, then conversation turned to the arrest of the former sheriff, Hilton Parks, which was still the talk of the town.

"So do you think he murdered that woman we found up on the mountain?" Wendy asked.

"I wouldn't put it past him," John Wilson replied. "He was going to let those guys set fire to that house while the sheriff and those women were in the basement. I can't believe he was the sheriff in this county for so long. Didn't anyone catch on to what a crook he was? I mean, even when his son was arrested, there were just too many questions left unanswered. I don't know the new sheriff, but it's no wonder she won the election. People were looking for someone fresh and new, and hopefully honest."

"I wonder if there is a local paper lying around here? Maybe there's something new since we were in town last," Wendy said, sliding out of the booth. "I'll see if Jo Ann has one tucked away somewhere."

She returned with a thick newspaper in hand. "No local paper, but she said there's some coverage in the Arizona Daily Times. Let's see what we can find."

She scattered out sections of the paper to each one at the table, keeping the front pages for herself. Other than the wildfire, they were no longer front page news, but she found a small blurb mid section. She read it, then passed it to Gwen to read. Gwen in turn passed her section of the paper to Wendy. She glanced through it, scanning the upscale houses and upscale Arizona living pages from Scottsdale.

"Look," Gwen said. "Here's a picture of that poor murdered woman's family. It's not a very good photo of the husband. Just a snapshot. He's got his cap pulled down over his face like he doesn't want anyone to see him. I'll bet she loved that." She smiled. "My dad used to do that. My mom would wait till the last minute and pull his cap off his head. In most of our family pictures Dad's swatting at Mom and the two of them have their mouths open." She sighed. "I love my family."

Wendy took the paper from her and squinted at the photo. "He looks kind of familiar." She handed the paper back to Gwen and continued to peruse her own section of the paper.

Suddenly she gasped. "Look!" She jabbed a finger at the page in front of her. "It's him! That's the guy."

"What guy?" Gwen asked, leaning over her shoulder to look.

"You know, the one we saw up there on the mountain before the fire. The one with the flat tire. The fisherman. The one who wasn't a fisherman. That Roger Smith guy."

Tom Sly leaned in from the opposite direction. "Yeah, I think you're right. Wow. I wonder what he was doing up here. No wonder he looked so out of place."

The paper went from Tom to John and then back to Wendy. They were still discussing the matter when Steve joined them with Bernie. "Hey, guys," he greeted, his dimples deepening and his face taking on slight rosy tint as embarrassment tinged his cheeks. "This is Deputy Bernie Fite. Bernie, the rest of my crew, John Wilson, Tom Sly, Wendy Thompson and Gwen Watson."

They shook hands all around. Gwen and Wendy slid further into the booth so that Bernie could join them.

"So, anything new in the paper? Steve asked.

"Not really," Wendy told him. "But, hey, you remember that guy we saw up behind the Big Lake Overflow Campground that day? About a week or so before the fire started. He had a flat tire, said he was fishing?"

"Yeah, I remember him. Roger Smith, right? What about him?"

"Well, look, his picture is in the paper!" She passed the paper across the table to him and pointed a finger.

Bernie leaned into the group. "You've seen this guy up here?" she asked.

They took turns telling Bernie about the man

they had encountered with the flat tire, each adding their own opinions as to why the man was in the mountains dressed like he'd just walked out of the office.

"When was this?"

"About a week before the Wallow Fire started," Gwen told her. "He said he was up there to meet some buddies for fishing, but he was several miles away from the lake, and there was no fishing gear to be seen anywhere. And he certainly wasn't dressed to fish."

"Wendy thought he was really sexy and good looking," Tom teased. Wendy swatted at his head.

"Did not, you idiot. He gave me the creeps." She shuddered.

Bernie gazed at the photo. "He is kind of good looking," she smiled watching Steve from the corner of her eye. "You know, in a funeral director kind of way."

Bernie grabbed the paper. She tucked the paper under her arm and stood up. "Come on, guys, you're all coming with me. Let's go see the sheriff."

Tossing money on the table to cover their breakfasts, they followed her out of the restaurant.

Bernie waited for the group to join her before entering the sheriff's office. No one was at the central desk. She indicated that they all should take a seat and crossed to the door that led to the holding cells. O.P. Barry met her in the hallway.

"Hey, Bernie. What's up?"

"Andee been around today?"

"Naw. I think she went to church with her folks."

———⸭⟨◉⟩⸭———

Andee felt her phone vibrate. She withdrew it from her pocket and opened her text messages. She could sense her mother frowning, but ignored it. It would take a while, even longer than eighteen months, for her mother to understand that being available was part of the job, even in church. She read Bernie's text with trepidation. *'Important info- murder- your office- now.'* She showed it to Morgan sitting beside her, then nudged her mother and whispered that she had to go. "Can't it wait?" her mother mouthed and she replied "no" before excusing herself and moving into the aisle.

She felt her mother's look of disapproval all the way out the door as she and Morgan moved as quietly as possible. At least the pastor was just starting his sermon, so they weren't interrupting him in the middle of it.

Morgan had met her at her house and they had

driven together to the church that morning. She unlocked her Jeep and they clambered aboard in silence. She quickly text *'On my way'*, before starting the engine and pulling out of the parking lot. "Bernie wouldn't have called me out of church over something trivial," she told Morgan.

They made their way to Main Street and turned left at the light. She pulled into the visitor's spot in front of the office and shut off the engine.

Bernie was standing before the five young firefighters when they entered the building. She smiled and left them to meet Andee and Morgan.

"Sorry to get you out of church," she said, "but I think you're going to want to hear this.

"This is the crew on Engine 62," she said by way of introduction. "They are the ones who found the body of Roma Montgomery. They also ran into someone about a week before they discovered her body that I think you will find interesting."

As if by unspoken consent, John Wilson, their captain on the crew, became their spokesperson. He explained how they had been out on patrol the week before the Wallow Fire had started and ran into a guy with two flat tires on the 68 Road behind the Big Lake Overflow Campground.

"We called for someone to come up and help him, but wasn't much more we could do. He said he was fishing, but the girls didn't think he was telling us the truth. He wasn't dressed like a fisherman."

"Did you get his name?"

"Well, he said his name was Roger Smith," Gwen said. Morgan and Andee exchanged glances.

"But now we know he was lying," Wendy said. She handed the paper to Andee. "It was this guy," she pointed.

Andee stared at the newspaper ad offering funeral and cremation services. She looked at Morgan. "Isn't this where Roma worked?"

Morgan's face was grim. He nodded. "And the slick...sonof... he let the rest of the epitaph escape silently, "almost got away with it."

"I need statements from all of you," she told the group. "Anything at all that you can remember. Bernie will take care of that. I've got a couple of calls to make. I'll be back in a bit."

She turned on her heel and headed for her office. Morgan followed. "I can't believe we were so far off," she exclaimed as she rounded her desk. She was already dialing her phone as she sit down.

"Detective Raymond, please."

A Sergeant Davidson informed her that Detective Raymond was not in. She left a message for the detective to call her as soon as possible and hung up.

Morgan hung up from the call he was making

and grinned at her. He pulled a pad from his shirt pocket and tore a page out of it.

"Look, Detective Raymond can do her thing down there once you've talked to her, but someone needs to talk to some of those witnesses at that convention. About twelve funeral directors from the Vegas-Henderson area said they attended the convention and listened to Rosencrans' speech. But this was all on Saturday. We all just assumed if he closed his business on Friday to go to the convention that he left on Friday and drove up there. But he could have killed her on Thursday night, driven up here, dumped the body and still have made it to Vegas in time for his speech. We need to talk to those directors. You take that half, I'll take this half. Can I use Sandra's desk?"

Andee was already dialing the phone as he left her office.

Thirty minutes later, she hung up on the last number on her list. The yellow legal pad in front of her was filled with notes. She had made contact with six of the eight directors on her list. Thankfully most funeral directors were connected to an answering service, because one never knew when the business of attending the dead would present itself. She left her office and joined Morgan. Bernie was ushering the firefighters out the door.

"Any luck?" Bernie asked.

Andee gave her a thumbs up and waited for Morgan to finish his phone call. She picked up the signed statements left by the firefighters. She walked to the wall behind Sandra's desk and pulled down a forest service road and topography map. Reading off the top of the stack, she found the road the firefighters said they were on and traced it over to the logging road on which Roma Montgomery had been found. As the crow flies, only about two miles, but in a vehicle, probably five. And far enough away from the body dump that no one would be suspicious, had he not had flat tires and needed help. For that matter, if he'd not placed an ad in the Arizona Daily Times, he might just have gotten away with murder. They were going to get this guy.

The phone rang and she cut a beeline to her office to answer. It was Detective Raymond returning her call.

"Sorry to bother you on a Sunday," Andee apologized.

"Murder happens every day of the week in my business," she said. "Sgt. Davidson said this was in regards to the Montgomery case?"

Andee filled her in, with the detective asking pertinent questions as she talked. "I sure never figured him for the murder," Raymond said. "Fax me those statements and I think with what you've told me we have enough to get a warrant. I'll see if I can find a judge who is willing to get me a warrant on Sunday morning. I'll pay him a visit this morning. I'll let you know what I find."

Andee joined Morgan and Bernie in the main office.

"The wheels are in motion," she told them. "Detective Raymond is going to try to find a judge and get a warrant. She'll let us know when it's done."

Chapter 26
Two days later
A Real Date

"What's up, Carlie?"

Carlie laughed. "Well, in lieu of our new suspect, I thought you'd want to know. The prints on the handle we found match the suspect. That small button I found in the body bag? It didn't come from the vic's clothing. It's a match to a shirt Frank Rosencrans picked up at the cleaners just before they arrested him. And the partial on it could be the suspect's as well."

"What was that handle, anyway?" Andee asked her.

"It's a casket handle. It screws on to a rod or an Allen wrench that is inserted into a small hole in the casket to lock and seal the casket."

"Hmm. We'd have had our suspect sooner if

we'd asked Bruce Botswell what the object was. I don't know. I sure never figured Roma's boss for the crime," Andee said. "I still think there is something fishy about Roger Montgomery, but maybe that's just because I know he was a wife beater."

She broke the connection and left her office. The Wallow Fire was winding down. The meteorologists were predicting monsoon. If monsoons hit with their usual vengeance in the mountains, there would be major flooding throughout the county. Volunteers were already placing sandbags in strategic areas. The National Forest was closed to all visitors until further notice. Officially, summer had just begun, but in the White Mountains of eastern Arizona, it was already over.

The towns in Apache County depended on their summer visitors. This could very well be one of the worst years yet for the economy of the county. All those wonderful plans the Chamber of Commerce had were a wash. It was still up in the air if they would try it again next summer. One could only hope.

She entered the Saw Mill Restaurant and made her way to the back table. Morgan and Bernie were waiting for her. She felt a small tinge of jealousy as she approached them. They seemed so comfortable together. She gave herself a mental shake and greeted them both warmly.

She gave Justin her order, and sipped the iced tea Bernie had ordered for her.

"So how was the trip up from the valley?" she asked Morgan.

"Uneventful, thankfully."

"I'm starving, so can we talk while we eat? I mean, if you don't mind me gobbling my food and talking with my mouth full. I haven't eaten since noon yesterday…" she let her voice trail off. "What?" she sputtered at Morgan. "I've been busy. Besides it won't hurt me to miss a meal now and then."

Bernie laughed. "Let's just let Morgan talk and you can eat as fast as you want in your unladylike manner."

Laughing, Morgan agreed.

Detective Raymond, he told them, had gotten a search warrant for the mortuary, the Rosencrans home and his automobiles. They had found blood in one of the hearses and it matched Roma's. Evidently Rosencrans killed her, put her in a body bag and left her in the hearse in the garage until he could rent another vehicle.

"But why did he kill her?" Andee blurted around a mouth full of hamburger.

Morgan smiled indulgently.

"Evidently Frank Rosencrans was in love with Roma Montgomery," he said.

Andee snorted, nearly choking on her food. She apologized and motioned for him to go on as she wiped her mouth."

According to Roma's friend, Selma, Rosencrans had been trying to talk her into leaving Roger for months.

"Really nice of Selma to tell us that when you questioned her," Andee said.

"I guess, like us, she just didn't figure Frank for the killer," Morgan defended. "But Detective Raymond gave her the third degree. I doubt she held anything back on that one." He chuckled. "That's one mean detective."

He continued. Roma had gone into work on Thursday morning with yet another black eye. Rosencrans was furious."

"But he is married, isn't he?" Andee asked popping another fry in her mouth.

Morgan shrugged. "I guess he isn't happily married."

According to friends he and his wife didn't get along. He's from a fairly wealthy family. They have a chain of hardware stores throughout the east coast. His father died when he was fourteen. He married her while he was still in college, studying for a business degree. She's one of those extreme-environmentalist-save-the-world-women and a bit of a socialite.

Evidently his wife and his mother thought he'd do the expected and run the family business. After they were married he decided to leave the family business, become a mortician and move to Arizona. She wasn't happy about the move or the business he chose.

"Selma told the detective that Frank had been coming on to Roma about six months after she started working for him. He gave her a loan to pay off the gambling debts Roger had made. Roma had warned him that she would file a sexual harassment suit against him, but Frank knew she wouldn't because she didn't want to upset Roger. For Roma, it was a Catch 22. Put up with Frank's declarations of love and sexual innuendos, or get beaten up by a jealous husband. Besides she owed him money and could not quit her job."

"So why did he kill her? I mean, if he loved her. How did it happen?

Morgan told them that after Detective Raymond found the blood in the hearse and the receipt where he'd rented a Jeep late Thursday evening, Frank came clean about everything.

He and Roma had been in the prep room cleaning instruments and getting ready to close up for the weekend. Frank had argued that since he was one of the speakers at the funeral directors' convention in Vegas, and she was planning to leave Roger that weekend, anyway, that they should go to Vegas and enjoy the weekend together.

Roma told him she was leaving Roger, but she wanted a clean slate when she did it. Frank said he couldn't change her mind, no matter what he said. He even threatened to fire her. She told him if she did she'd have his license. She said that after Roger was out of the picture she would have no problems going to the authorities and charging him with sexual harassment. Frank said he got really angry. He was offering her everything. His love, his business, his money.

She told him she was leaving. He pushed her. She shoved past him, trying to leave the room. He grabbed her and swung her around. He was holding a scalpel in hand and she lost her balance and fell against it. He said he hadn't realized he had stabbed her because she kept hitting him in the face and screaming at him. He didn't know how to shut her up so he could talk to her, so he slapped her. That seemed to make her want to fight more. He grabbed her around the neck and started choking her. By the time he realized what he was doing, it was too late and she was dead.

Frank panicked. He knew she wouldn't be missed until Sunday night, but he didn't want anyone to find her body at his place of business. He knew he would be the number one suspect. He called a car rental about six miles away, requested a four-wheel drive and they delivered him a Jeep Cherokee. As fate would have it, the spare tire was flat so when the Jeep got a flat tire on the mountain he couldn't beat a hasty retreat as he had planned.

He dropped the rental off in Show Low, rented another vehicle with his wife's credit card. He said they used to laugh about there being two Frank Rosencrans. He drove straight through to Vegas that night, arriving about one in the morning. He hadn't stayed at the MGM because he was hoping Roma would agree to go with him and he thought she would be more comfortable somewhere they wouldn't be recognized.

"He joined the other funeral directors for breakfast the next morning and went through the day as if things were normal. He had all weekend to come up with a story to tell the police when he called to tell them he'd found evidence of foul play at his mortuary. If he hadn't had those flat tires when he dumped her body, he probably would never have been recognized nor caught.

"But why did he bring her all the way up here?" Bernie asked. "Why not just take her out in the desert and dump her? There's a lot of desert down there. She might not have been found for months. That's just weird since the other women were kidnapped and brought up here. Do you think he knew that?"

Morgan shook his head. "As far as we know, there's no connection to Parks. But he does have a connection to the mountain. He has a cousin over in St. Johns. He actually works for our esteemed sheriff."

Bernie and Andee gaped at him.

"Who?" they asked in unison.

"Tubby O'Toole."

"No!" Andee choked. "Seriously?"

"Seriously," Morgan told her.

"So did Tubby know anything about his cousin's activities?"

"Evidently not. But we figure that's why Rosencrans chose this area. He'd been up here a time or two and figured some of those back roads would hide his crime until the wild animals destroyed the evidence.

"He had talked to a director from the funeral home where one of the women was taken. That was how he learned about the case files, but evidently they didn't go into detail when they told him about it."

Morgan continued with his story.

Frank rented the jeep, loaded her body into it and drove up the mountain on Thursday night. He wasn't expected to be in the mortuary on Friday, and didn't have to speak at the convention until Saturday. More than enough time to dump the body and get to

Las Vegas before anyone was the wiser. It was just a stroke of bad luck that he found himself with two flat tires. That threw a kink in his well laid plans.

"How is the Montgomery family taking the news?" Andee asked.

"The oldest boy seems to be quite relieved that his dad didn't kill his mom," Morgan said. "I talked to him briefly outside his grandmother's house. He said he was glad his dad was moving away and that he and his siblings were going to stay with their grandmother until he found a place to settle. That's got to be a huge burden, suspecting you father killed your mother. I think he was reluctant to put his siblings in the same house with his father, not knowing for sure."

"I still can't believe Roger had nothing to do with it. There's something about that man that doesn't gel with me."

"He's just not a very nice guy," Bernie laughed. "But you haven't met Frank. To hear Gwen and Wendy talk, he is the epitome of creep. Wendy said she felt like he'd crawled out from under a rock and was lying in wait to 'slime' someone."

"But I saw the picture in the paper. He didn't look creepy," Andee said. "In fact he was kind of a nice looking guy."

"I guess you had to be there and talk to him," Bernie shrugged.

"Detective Raymond has put together a pretty intense profile of the guy," Morgan said. "I guess he's not as lily white as he would have the world believe. He had a series of misdemeanors as a teen. One of his girlfriends disappeared while he was in college. They are reopening that investigation. There were a couple of old complaints on file in Maricopa County, about how he handled business at the mortuary, but they'd been dropped before anything came of them. Turns out he had offered some veiled threats to the people who complained and then offered free burial services if they would drop the charges."

"Wow. Really nice guy, huh?" Andee pushed her plate back and wiped crumbs away. "So Parks won't be taking the hit for the murder of Roma Montgomery."

"He's in so much trouble with all the stuff he's done, he'll never be a free man," Bernie said.

Jason came and cleared their plates and left their bills. They talked for another fifteen minutes before pushing back their chairs and leaving the restaurant.

Morgan and Andee stood waiting just outside the restaurant door for Bernie to pay her bill.

"What's the rest of your day look like?" Morgan asked her.

She shrugged. "Some paperwork. Checking in with the troops. I'm supposed to be off for the weekend. I haven't had a weekend off since this fire started. I'm thinking it will be a few weeks before I see any more time off. Why?"

"Well," he grinned. "Since we both agree that you owe me, *big time*, I thought you might want to go get a steak over in Show Low tonight."

"Hmmm. Since I owe you huh? Does that mean I'm buying?"

"Maybe. I'd intended to pay but since you owe me..." He hesitated. "Actually," he said, "I was thinking along the lines of a real date, and in that case, it would behoove me to pay."

Andee pursed her lips. "I see. A real date." She smiled across at him. "It's been a while since I've been on a real date. I might embarrass you."

"I'll take my chances."

"Well, in that case," she laughed, "I would love to go on a real date with you, Morgan Freeman."

Bernie joined them and Morgan headed for his truck. "I'll call you," he said with a wave.

Bernie pulled her sunglasses down on her nose and looked over the top of them at Andee. Andee blushed and pulled her keys from her pocket. "We're going on a date," she said smugly. "A real date."

She climbed into the Tahoe and pulled out of the parking lot, leaving Bernie staring after her with a big smile on her face.

*Wallow Fire Statistics:

The Wallow Fire was started on May 29, 2011
It was 100% contained July 8, 2011.
Total burned: 538,049 acres, 817 square miles in Arizona
15,407 acres, 24 square miles in New Mexico
10,000 people were evacuated, 500 elected to stay behind
16 injuries, no deaths
32 residences destroyed, 5 damaged
4 commercial buildings destroyed
36 out-buildings destroyed, 1 damaged
1 vehicle destroyed
There were 19 red flag (no fire) days before May 29, 2011. Wind gusts were over 60 mph.

Monsoon did not end problems for the communities affected by the Wallow Fire. The rains brought severe flooding in many areas including Alpine, Nutrioso, Greer and parts of South Eagar. It has been determined that flooding will continue to be a major problem for several years to come.

Cost to fight Wallow Fire: $109 million

The fire was started accidentally by two men who were camping. They cooperated with prosecutors and plead guilty to misdemeanor charges relating to mismanagement of their campfire. In November, 2012 they were ordered to pay restitution in the amount of $3.7 million.

*http://www.inciweb.org/incident/2262/

CPSIA information can be obtained at www.ICGtesting.com
Printed in the USA
BVOW05s2016060814

361907BV00001B/2/P